'Such a ████████████████████ otions,
followed by a mix of mythical and mystical.'

Hannah Gold, Waterstones Book Prize 2022 Winner

Also by Finbar Hawkins

Witch

FINBAR HAWKINS

ZEPHYR

An imprint of Head of Zeus

First published in the UK in 2022 by Zephyr, an imprint of Head of Zeus
This Zephyr paperback edition first published in the UK in 2023 by Head of Zeus,
part of Bloomsbury Publishing Plc

975312468

A catalogue record for this book is available from
the British Library.

ISBN (PB): 9781838935658
ISBN (E): 9781838935665

Typeset and designed by Jessie Price / Head of Zeus

Printed and bound in Great Britain
by CPI Group (UK) Ltd, Croydon CR0 4YY

Head of Zeus
5–8 Hardwick Street
London EC1R 4RG
WWW.HEADOFZEUS.COM

To my parents, Colin & Jacqui,
for everything.

'The horse carried a warrior not only into battle, but also into the afterlife.'

David Miles, *The Land of the White Horse* (2019)

XIII ◉ DEATH

Dad went to the desert one day and never came back.

He was driving his squad through the centre of Kabul. It was a routine morning thing, and they were passing through a busy market, when the suicide bomber struck.

A car packed with explosives rammed their truck, killing them all.

Ten civilians also lost their lives.

And tomorrow we bury him.

My dad, who went to that desert, who never said goodbye to me.

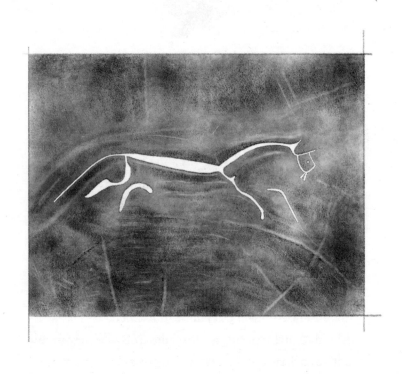

C had said there was a party at Darren's, his folks were away. Spot on. That's what I needed. Mum wasn't pleased.

'It's your dad's funeral in the morning, Sam.'

'Exactly, Mum.' I open the door, and I'm out of there, before she can say another word.

There are girls dancing in a darkened room. Lads watching from the bright kitchen, too cool, too shy. Timbo, Sharkey and Ben. They've got ciders on the go. I swipe one, expecting it to be grabbed back, but nobody's bothered, too high on the *thrum thrum thrum* from that room.

There's Chloe, and Tash by her side, as always. And May and moody Gina. They're laughing, swaying to the music. And then I see this girl I've not seen before.

'Now, who's that?' says Chad.

Sharkey doesn't turn, flicking his long hair over his can.

'Oona something,' he slurs. 'Family's just arrived from barracks in Germany.'

I swig, feeling the sour tang hit my belly. Don't really like cider, but I don't want to stand out.

'Sam!' Chad leans across. 'Come dance.'

'No, I don't—'

The girls shriek with laughter. I turn to see they're looking this way. The music changes, *mum-mum-mum, ahhing* off the walls and I catch the unknown girl's eye, a black flash, as the others pull her into their dance. I like this song, working its magic on me. Or is it her, Oona Something?

'Classic, Sam! Come on!' Chad's pulling me too, and I don't want to, not if they're all watching, but she's there, and I want to get closer.

'Whoop! Whoop! Come on!'

I see Chloe and Tash swap looks as we enter the press of that room. Everyone's here for me, but nobody knows what to say. I don't want them to say anything. I just want them to be normal. Chloe smiles and turns up the volume and we cheer, letting the music enfold us.

The girl with the huge eyes throws shapes, her shadow leaping on the wall. Chad's grinning, as he sidles between Chloe and Tash, and I'm laughing, at how good it feels, how nothing matters here. But then I find myself standing off and watching them, feel my smile ache. They crouch, singing together.

I see Oona smiling as she pushes back her long hair, she mouths the words, that everyone shouts,

'*Oh, whoa, oh oh, oh, oh oh...*'

Chad has gone into a conga with Chloe, spinning between the girls who are all laughing at him, the clown.

The room shakes, as Chad moves towards Oona. I can't take my eyes off them, dancing closer and closer, but now Chloe is watching like me.

Over Chad's shoulder, Oona shoots me a look, a dark arrow of eyes that stop me dead. Chad leans in to speak to her, this girl who smiles at me. She replies, and Chad can't hear of course, and *isn't that funny*.

The music and bodies move around them, and I want to go forward and say something to her, push Chad out of the way, so I can see her smile at me again.

Oona laughs as Chad pulls a face. And Chloe is staring like me, because she's thinking, thinking of Chad, we all know she's thinking of Chad.

Oona glances at him, then back at me. She looks down as she dances and it's as if she's in slow motion, smiling to the music. She's so very beautiful.

Sharkey knocks into me, shouting. But I'm frozen to the spot. I can't do a thing, just watch. I'm stuck. Stuck for ever.

Chad's leaning close to Oona. Her head turned towards him.

I can't be here anymore. I shouldn't have come.

I push past Sharkey, sloshing his drink.

I barge through Chad and Oona, glad to spoil their fun.

'Sam?'

Chloe jumps clear.

'All right! Slow down!'

I don't, and I don't care as I stumble against moody Gina, wrench the back doors open, dive into the dark.

I throw my hands out, my knuckles scrape the wall, and the pain only makes me more furious. I want to hit something really hard.

I glance around the little garden, a security light burns my eyes. Garden stuff, a plastic sandpit, a chair and a mauled football. I whack it against the wall.

I sit on the chair, breathing, breathing, trying to catch my breath.

Thinking of the girl called Oona I couldn't talk to.

Thinking of my best friend Chad who could.

Thinking, why can't I be more like him?

Thinking what Dad would say.

'Hey...'

Oona moves into the garden, light touching the tips of her hair.

'Are you okay?'

I nod as I look at her face in the glare, and her immense

eyes swallow me whole. Her skin is so white and clear, and those freckles splash across her nose and cheeks. A single eyebrow rises under a few falling strands of her hair. And I don't know why, I just want to take her hand, open the back gate and run away from this party, this town, this place.

'I'm Oona, by the way.'

'I know.'

That eyebrow raises again.

'Little bit stalkery, Sam…'

The laugh jumps out of me.

'Yeah, sorry… I heard… just like you heard… Someone said… your name…' I can't get my words to behave, all jostling to impress her.

She smiles. 'It's freezing out here. Shall we—'

'No! Not back in there.'

Oona looks down at my hand holding hers. I didn't know I had grabbed it. She takes a step closer, eyes searching mine, eyes that see me and only me. My hand trembles. Like my lip.

'You're not okay, are you? Has something happened?'

How do I begin to answer that? I look at her hand that still holds mine, and think about running again. How far would we get? Before everything caught up with us.

'Yeah…' I say and whisper, 'My…'

I'm shaking now, but I'm not cold, as Oona kneels and rubs my hand, my arm. She touches my face, the tears I didn't know were there.

'Oh, Sam, *shush* now. Oh, Sam… *shush*, what is it, you can tell me, *shush* now…'

And I can, can't I? I can tell this unknown girl. Who I feel I could trust with everything, my life pushed into those warm, soft hands that stroke my face.

'My dad.'

I shake again, tears flowing. I'm like a toddler blubbing to his mum, all I need to do is cry and cry, until everything is all right, until she makes it better. She nods and goes, *shush, shush*, drawing it from me, this terrible thing I can't hold anymore.

'My dad's…'

A sound behind us. A cough. We both look round, and Chad is there, and he looks at me crying, at Oona close to me, my hands in hers.

'Sam, man…'

He steps forward and my belly hardens. I can't help it.

'Oh, Chad, how great to see you!'

I stand, wiping those tears away.

'Sammy…'

'Had a good dance, did you?'

Oona's looking at us both.

'Sam, come on…'

His voice is calm and friendly. He reaches for me, but I flick his hand away.

'Sam, man, let's…'

'No, let's not, Chad, *man*!'

I can't help it again. Chad's my best mate. He's done

nothing wrong. A bit of dancing and flirting. That's what Chad does. That's why everyone likes him. That's why Oona likes him.

'Let's have a game of keepy-uppy instead, eh?'

I roll the manky football onto my foot, toe it and grab it out of the air. Chad watches me. Oona watches me.

'Sam, just calm...'

'Catch!'

I kick that ball, as if I'm kicking him, and Chad slips. The ball whams into the garage.

'Sam! What you doing?'

He looks at me through that mop of hair.

'I'm going home, Chad. What *you* doing?'

And I kick the ball so it whams again.

Then I turn from them both, from my mate who's good and charming, from the girl with the blackest eyes, the girl who cared.

I leave them behind in that cold garden, and disappear into the night.

'I'm tired, Dad, I can't walk anymore!'

'Okay, matey – how about a ride on the horse's back?'

He bends down, dropping his knapsack.

'Climb aboard, captain.'

I hold onto his shoulders and swing on, and Dad scoots my bum back, folding my legs under his arms.

'Ready? Then we're off!'

I giggle as he starts to canter through the grass.

'Keep watching ahead, Sammy – we should see it soon!'

I look over his shoulder as he neighs like a horse and tosses his mane.

'Dad!' I laugh.

'What can you see?' He asks the question.

'A long hill, going up high.' I give the answer. Our little ritual. Just ours.

'Good, that means we're close!'

We canter on, a few people cluster on the hillside, cagoules and walking boots. Dad said the White Horse has been a tourist spot for centuries, for everyone coming to pay homage to that galloping, prancing guardian of the hill.

We make the top, and the wind rushes up, makes me catch my breath. And it's strange, it's completely flat here, a huge circle of land. A few people are standing on the bank, pointing and looking out.

'The Iron Age hill fort, Sam – this is where it would have been….'

I follow where he's pointing, imagining the wooden walls of the old fort. And as Dad talks, I see them, as though he's conjured them through time, villagers trotting to and fro. A goose pecking in

the dirt. Sentries keeping a watchful eye, until one of them hollers. An attack! A surge of an army climbing towards them...

'Come on, it's over here! Giddy up!'

Dadhorse neighs and races across the green plain. A couple stop and stare.

'Dad! People think you're mad!'

'Who cares?' He gallops faster. 'Who cares when we've got the White Horse to see!'

We make the edge of the ridge and the world spills beneath us. Field upon field, and here and there, hills bump into a giant patchwork blanket that stretches across the land. Two birds hover against the clouds, strong wings defying the wind.

'Kites...' Dad checks himself. 'No. Ravens. Funny, you don't see them up here much.'

One calls, twisting and falling, then swooping steady. I know from Dad that ravens aren't predators, but still I feel its beady, killer eyes on me, willing me to bolt.

'And here... Here we are at last...'

Dad points. An edge of white chalk gouged into the turf.

'Where's the horse, Dad?'

He laughs, hoists me higher onto his shoulders.

'Can you see it better now? I bet those birds have got the best view.'

I pull myself above Dad's head and peer down. I can make out a little more. A nose, an eye, the curve of a leaping leg. But I can't see it all. I look up at the watching ravens as they judder in the wind.

'Why did they make it, Dad? If they couldn't see it...'

'Ah, but if you're over there...' *Dad sets me down and points across the land,* 'on those hills, or in those woods, then you'd see it, sure enough. A huge, great horse always running.'

I imagine the people, then, coming from miles and miles to stop and stare.

'Can we go there?'

'Surely, Sam... Surely.' *He ruffles my hair as the ravens call, and something makes me turn towards the hill. A tall, bearded man stands, with two mighty dogs, brindled beasts. The wind catches his flowing hair.*

'Dad – look at that man.'

Dad turns and looks. The man lifts his hand to the sky. And Dad waves.

'Do you know him, Dad?'

The man is walking, striding, and now I can see that he's got a long stick, a staff in one hand.

'No. He's got big dogs, hasn't he? Alsatians, I think...'

The man lifts both his hands to the sky. He's summoning something. Something high above us.

'Dad! Look, the ravens!'

They spiral and screech, coursing the wind, and as we watch, they plunge down, down towards the man's outstretched arms, two shadows that swirl about him.

'Well, I'll be...' *Dad stares as the man turns, the birds*

flapping close, the huge hounds at his side. 'Must be an animal trainer or something...'

Dad is quiet, as the man on the hill lifts his staff. It's funny, it's as if he's calling to us now.

'Shall we wave, Sam?' Dad kneels beside me 'Maybe he'll bring us luck.'

He cups his hand and bellows.

'Hello! Hello!' He raises his arm to wave, and as I watch, the man on the hill waves back.

'He is waving, Dad! He is waving!'

'Go on, then, say hello!'

I lift my hand, but a shiver runs through me. I don't wave. Instead I watch Dad, smiling and waving to the animal man with his birds and dogs, until he disappears below the ridge. Until we can see only his hair rising, lifting, a single raven hangs high then drops, and they are gone.

And we're left, just me and Dad and the wind.

XIII • DEATH

I jolt awake.

Grey light edges the curtains, showing this strange object that's landed in our house, like an alien from outer space.

I follow the grain of its wood, the polished silver handles, the ring of flowers Mum has placed around a silver plate, and I read those engraved words:

ALAN MITCHELL, SERGEANT-AT-ARMS,
2ND BATTALION THE RIFLES, 1972-2020

Dad's in there.

But then he's not. More dust than Dad.

I check my phone. 5.47 a.m. There's a missed call and a text.

Call me! You still suck at footie. Chad.

I remember. The party.

Wanting to be there, and not wanting to be there, wanting to hit something.

The unknown girl. Oona Something, smiling her freckled smile.

Chad's face when he saw us.

The slam of the ball into metal.

I sit quickly, and knock something over. A can of beer spills. I rub it with my foot. Dad's beer. I found some old cans, waiting and warm.

Warm like Oona's hands on my face.

But I'd run, crying like a baby, leaving her and Chad. Why did I do that?

Another car passes, its headlights sweep the coffin, catch the photos on the sideboard.

Beth and me in the garden.

I'm seven, she's five. I'm in my stripy trunks, pulling a pose, milk teeth missing. Beth's in a tutu, waving a plastic wand. The princess and the strongman.

There's Mum and Dad at a taverna table with suntan smiles and mad cocktails. Dad's eyes twinkling, as if to say,

So what was all that then with Chad? He's your best bud.

I don't know, Dad. I just got... I don't know.

You got jealous.

There he is in his Rifles uniform, full regalia and camouflage.

Oona. Nice Irish name.

Birds are singing outside. I feel drained.

I love you, Dad.

More than salt?

That fairy tale he used to read me with the princess who tells her father how much she loves him. I kiss my fingertips and press them to Dad's cheek.

'More than salt, Dad,' I whisper in that grey light, 'more than salt,' and I climb the stairs to bed.

I pause on the landing and glimpse Mum in the kitchen, dressed in a new black suit, bought specially for today. A shroud to join the flock of other specially bought clothes. Death is like a celebrity with all this fuss and attention. My phone buzzes. A number I don't know.

Sam, I heard about today.

And your dad. I'm really sorry.

I got your number from Beth btw.

See you in school.

Oona

I stare at the message, at her name, remembering her eyes flashing black as can be. How she'd followed me outside. Held me when I'd started shaking. No girl's ever done that before.

Aw, Sam, you're so shy and sweet. Tash and Chloe always teasing me.

Sam, you ever been kissed? Them laughing, holding onto each other.

Not by me he hasn't!

Nor me!

'Sammy, love?'

How thin Mum looks. Her hair, threaded with grey, is tied in a bun. She reminds me of a picture I saw in History of a Spanish woman, weeping over the body of a fallen solider. She sees me, cocking her head to one side, she tries to smile, but it's as if she's forgotten how to.

'There's some breakfast here...'

A cup of tea and some toast. Steam rises from the mug, curling in the morning light. I don't want to eat. But I don't want to upset Mum. I sit, as she moves like a quick black bird about the kitchen. She wipes crumbs, tidies cupboards, puts plates into the washing-up bowl. Then she looks out of the kitchen window, and I know she's searching for something to say, anything to say.

'October's not far. I'll miss those bossy blackcaps on the feeder...'

She tries to smile again, scrubbing at the plates harder. I see the shock slapped into her face.

'Mum...'

And I'm at her side, catching her, as she seems to slump. I feel her shuddering as she moves her head into my shoulder, burying her silent cry.

'I've got you, Mum, I've got you...'

She clutches me tight and I see a mug among the suds. It's the one that Beth made Dad as a jokey Christmas present. A picture of them blowing kisses in a photo booth under cheesy heavy metal style words, 'Dads & Daughters Rock!'

I hold Mum closer, soaking her sobs, then out of the window I see Maisy, the little girl next door. She's watching us from the top of her slide, a finger in her mouth.

This is what it's going to be like all day. People gazing at our grief, dumbstruck by Death. I shoo a hand at her, and can't help glaring. Maisy blinks then smiles and gives a big wave as she slides away, and if it wasn't for me holding onto Mum I would laugh out loud, for the stupidity of it all, for this little girl blundering into our day.

The kitchen door creaks. Beth's standing there, looking immaculate in a black velvet dress and matching headband. Her lipstick is bright red, those Egyptian queen flicks from her eyes like little black wings. Warpaint for what lies ahead.

'Hi,' she says and takes a step closer, reaching for Mum.

'Oh no, you'll set me off again!'

Mum puts her hand to Beth's face, not wanting her to be upset, and smiles that broken smile again.

'Mum, it's okay...'

'I'm fine, Beth, I'm fine, love. But I look a state,' she smooths her hair, catching her reflection in the window, 'they'll be here any minute,' and darts into the downstairs loo.

Beth and I watch her close the door on us.

I don't blame Mum. Given the full-on family we're about to face, I could easily stay in the bathroom all day.

Beth takes a bite out of my toast and winks at me. She's so Dad, she doesn't even know it. I follow her into the living room. It's filled with sunlight, and we both stand and watch the dust drift above Dad's coffin.

'Look! God!' we say together and crack up, because of course it's another Dad thing. It's what he would always say when we walked with him up on the Ridgeway, and the sun did that beautiful thing, sending down its rays of biblical light. Another piece of Dad, like his mug in dirty dishwater. His beer. His photos. We're surrounded by him. And he grins on, his arms around me and Beth as he points to where the shadows of the clouds break.

Look! God!

I watch Beth take Dad's army picture off the wall, cradling it before she places it gently near the flowers on his coffin. She turns it slightly so he's facing the window, as if he can watch the road, waiting patiently for his ride to arrive.

'You were back late, party boy. How was it?'

She strokes the lapel on my new jacket, and picks away a piece of cotton with one of her painted nails, a Mexican Day of the Dead skull, white on purple.

'It was…' I breathe, remembering how things were great, then how things weren't so great. 'It was okay.'

Beth's green eyes narrow.

'More than okay, if there's a girl chasing you.' She presses her hand to my chest where my heart beats a little faster. 'Oh yes, we can see into your soul, young Sam.' She twirls a talon and purrs. 'For we share our witchy ways, you know, me and a girl called… Oona.'

I start at her name, seeing her perfect smile, feeling her touch my face.

'Oonaahh…' Beth breathes, batting her eyelids. My younger sister. Older in her wisdom and wit than me.

'So tell me all. Or did she steal your tongue with her sweet ki—'

Two shadows pass the window and stop. Black cars, waiting. As we watch, doors open and figures step out, ghosting towards our door.

One of those cars is a hearse. Here to tell us where we are, what this day is, what must be done.

'Sam…'

Beth's eyes aren't playing anymore, they shine with fear. I take her hand in mine, pressing it hard.

'For Mum, Beth…'

I can't face her being sad. She doesn't realise how much I need her to be Beth right now. Because if she doesn't make it, then I'm lost.

'We need to be strong for her, Beth.'

She looks at me, and I see her wrestling the ache in her heart, until she nods just as our front door knocker creaks and falls twice. Not loudly, but respectfully, with sincerest condolences, enough to let us know they're here for Dad.

And from behind the bathroom door, we hear Mum sobbing.

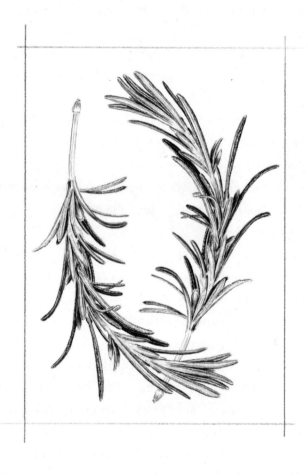

D ad's coffin creaks as four quiet men in long black coats lift it slowly, turning that oblong box for a body through the morning light. I hold on to my mother and my sister as, like me, they watch in silence.

'Come on, Mum, Bethy.'

We become a small procession to the front door where the quiet men place Dad's coffin in the hearse. Is Dad really in there? How can we be sure? In science, Mr Arnold told us this 'Schrodinger's Cat' thing. Quantum physics says that a cat in a box is both alive and dead because we cannot see it.

'Schrodinger suggests we place a radioactive sample, a Geiger counter and a bottle of poison in with poor puss...'

Mr Arnold's voice booms through my head as we arrange ourselves on the back seat. One of the funeral guys stifles a yawn.

'As the Geiger counter detects the sample decaying, it

triggers the smashing of the poison, and the cat dies…'

The hearse starts up. Mum is between me and Beth, so we can protect her from this headlong pile-up of a day.

'In conclusion, class – something is very definitely dead or alive, whether or not we open up the box to check.'

I think about the box in the hearse ahead. About Dad inside. Definitely dead. If he was alive, he would turn and laugh, 'Cheer up, you miserable lot. Who died, eh?'

Then he'd drive us to his favourite pub with a view of White Horse Hill, and tell us the stories that we've heard so many times, that we never tired of hearing.

As we move away, I glance up at that far hill where we used to climb with him. A few people are dotted about. And there, at the top, a walker strides beneath wheeling birds, dogs running ahead. He stops, as if taking in our convoy. A tall form, still against the massing clouds, till the trees and houses pass between us, and he's gone, a silhouette in my mind.

People watch us pass. Boys on bikes. Old ladies chatting. A mum with a pushchair. We turn the corner from our close, and there are people from school. Chloe and Tash giving sad smiles. Timbo raising his fist, warrior-style. Then, with a jolt, I see Chad and next to him, Oona. Chad mouths, 'See you there.' Oona looks at me, black eyes full of sadness and care.

'Rosemary,' says Beth.

'What?'

'Oona. She's holding a sprig of rosemary. Did you

know, the Romans believed it symbolised eternity?' Her
smile trembles. 'That death is a journey.'

I crane around as the car drives on.

Oona steps into the road. I see Chad reaching for her.

Thank God, I bet they're thinking. Thank God it's not
me in there. Because I've got stuff to do, life to lead.

Thank God I'm alive and not dead like poor Sam's dad.
Thank God. Thank God. Thank God.

The church steeple towers above us, jabbing the sky.

I used to love coming here with Gran when I was little.
The story of Christ on the walls. Gran's eyes closed after
Communion, her wrinkled hands clasped in prayer.

But there's no Gran anymore to give me a humbug and
tell me it will be all right.

Instead there are clusters of people, waiting for it all
to start.

Four soldiers are at the hearse, one I know, a pal of
Dad's, Charlie. He gives the others the nod and they
reach and carefully, respectfully lift Dad's coffin.

As we stand, like mournful sheep, Charlie's eyes meet
mine: *I'm with you, son.*

'Sam.'

Beth's voice in my ear. My eyes are blurry.

'Let's do this...' She squeezes my arm.

'... for Mum.'

I feel odd. Tired.

'Are you okay?'

My little sister. She's five, kneeling down to me where I've fallen from my bike. Bethy always looking out for me, squinting through her fringe.

'Yeah...' I clear my throat and look at Mum.

She's staring straight ahead, black gloves gripping black handbag. Beth and I move beside her, and together, we enter the dark mouth of the church.

Organ music floats above the heads of the congregation, full of mutters and murmurs. As we pass, people do that nod or half-smile thing, a few mouth our names. 'Beth...' 'Sam...' 'Sheila...' A sea of whispering well-meaning washes over us, but we don't stop, we walk on, to the front where Dad's coffin waits on a stand, for all to see. And next to his body, the photo of him in his uniform, grinning out at us.

'Here...'

Beth tugs me into the front pew with its 'Reserved' sign. Priority seats for the main event.

The priest in his white gown and green stole blinks through thick glasses. The organ music stops, and the silence fills with coughs that echo off the stone-cold walls.

'Peace be with you.' The priest makes the sign of the cross.

'And also with you.'

'We are gathered here today to celebrate the life of Alan Mitchell, much-loved husband to Sheila...' he nods to Mum, who bites her lip, 'loving father to Sam and Beth. Alan was a much-respected Sergeant Fusilier in...'

The priest's voice sounds on as I look down. The church floor has tiny sparkles in it, like stars shining in mist.

I feel like falling into them.

Into some other universe.

Somewhere far from here.

Dad told me once about 'Samhain', the old Irish name for the place between our world and the spirit world. Samhain.

It's Gaelic, Sam – pronounced 'Sow-in'.

But whenever I see that word, it reminds me of you, how magic you are to me...

That's the place, Dad. One-way ticket, please.

'It's time, Sam.' Beth nudges me. 'You need to...' She presses something into my hand.

The Order of Service. My turn to read.

So I stand, slipping from Beth and Mum, not wanting to leave them. I pause in the empty aisle, then make my way to the pulpit, where Father Blink smiles as he steps aside.

I see rows of faces, some I know, others I barely remember.

Dad's brother Patrick, burly and red, and Dad's mum, ancient and frail.

Dad's mates from the village.

Charlie and the soldiers.

And beside me Dad, still definitely dead.

I open the Order of Service. My hands shake. I can see my name next to a prayer. Lambs and Gods and Fathers. But there's nothing of *my* father there.

Light streams gold and red and blue from high windows, and I'm little again, next to Gran, as she's whispering her prayer, and I'm watching those colours move in the air.

Then I know. I know what Dad would like to hear.

The congregation watches, as I step from the pulpit, leave the prayer and go to where he lies, to stroke the smooth wood of his coffin, to know he's there, and that this is for him. I look up to those beautiful windows, and I start to sing,

'I've been a wild rover for many a year
And I spent all my money on whisky and beer...'

My voice soars making heads twitch and turn, because this isn't the Order of Service, this isn't funeral gloom and doom. But I don't care. I'm singing this for Dad. I'm singing as loud as I can, so he'll hear from inside his box, from across the dark sea, from deep in the desert far from me.

'But now I'm returning with gold in great store
And I never will play the wild rover no more...'

Mum's looking at me, she remembers Dad singing this. Then Beth is in the aisle, and I'm thinking one day she might marry, and Dad will never give her away. But she's by my side now, as she joins our song for our father.

'*And it's no, nay, never, no nay never no more,*
Will I play the wild rover, no never no more!'

We give it everything, till we can sing no more and I hug Beth, breathing in her laugh, her sob. I grip her close, wishing we could scoop Mum up, like superheroes and power blast through the steeple, rocket up, up and away.

But a hand on my shoulder brings us back to earth.

'Thank you, Sam...' the priest's tongue darts over his thin lips, and I'm reminded of a snake, 'that wass very sspecial.'

I guide Beth back to our seats, and in the hush Uncle Patrick honks into a hanky, and Charlie gives me a thumbs-up, as Mum clutches for us.

'He would have loved that... I didn't know you could sing, Sam!'

'Neither did I, Mum. Neither did I.'

We laugh into a huddle, our heads knocking, and it would be nice, wouldn't it, to emerge and see that everyone had gone, or that another ritual was waiting to start, a christening or a wedding, a gospel choir? But we are still at Dad's funeral, there's no hiding from it. The show must go on.

Readings are read, songs sung, prayers offered, as Mum, Beth and I sit through it, as the processing of Dad goes on.

Mum's gloved hand is wrapped in mine, Beth's tight in my other. I look at Dad's coffin and can almost hear his muffled chuckle,

You're the last man standing, son. You're surrounded.

Then Charlie and his sombre platoon are there, easing the coffin onto their camouflaged shoulders, as the organ starts to moan again. We rise, dumb with death and follow.

The congregation does its thing as we pass, and we all file out through the arched doorway into the light, behind those soldiers, who bear Dad aloft like he's their brand-new missile.

The sky above the cemetery is so blue, and birds bob here and there among the autumn trees. As we gather at the waiting grave, I remember the dream that has always stayed with me, the one I had after Gran died. We were walking, like this, behind her coffin. I remember Mum's face as she followed. I'd never seen her cry. But as I walked, Gran's coffin sprouted huge white flapping wings and lifted into the air soaring above the church. I remember it turned above the steeple. Its silver handles caught in a bright ray of sun, and Gran's great flying coffin followed that light, like a path into the clouds, until it was gone.

A blackbird flits on to a headstone, a little herald singing his fierce song,

'Cheer up! Cheer up now! You're nearly done! Nearly done!'

He's right. We're crowded round the solemn soldiers lowering Dad's coffin on long green ribbons. The priest shakes holy water. We're standing next to the pile of earth that will soon bury Dad.

'May his soul and the souls of all the faithful departed through the mercy of God rest in peace.'

The blackbird chirrups.

'Lamb of God, you take away the sins of the world – have mercy upon us.'

The priest throws earth into the grave, as if he's feeding a hungry mouth.

'Ashes to ashes...

...dust to dust.'

People toss more earth down on Dad, hypnotised by the sing-song prayer. Mum stoops too, and for a second, I think she's going to fall into the grave, to be buried with Dad, an ancient king and queen.

She scatters soil down into the dark, and again, and again, till Beth and I close in, bring her back from the brink.

'Come on, Mum...'

Beth puts her arm around her, and we turn from Dad's grave, leaving him in the ground, where the blackbird flutters and sings over the priest's last words,

'Go in peace. Amen.'

A wind rustles the turning leaves on the trees above us. Gold-tinged, orange and brown.

Would you look at that. You know, it's my favourite time of the year...

Yes, Dad, we know. You say it every time.

An usher stands at the cemetery gate, Border Control for the bereaved.

With a lowering of his head, he steers us to the car, and we fall into it. The usher doesn't look at us as he closes the door. The driver doesn't say a word as the car moves away.

Because what is there to say?

Only that he's gone.

That he's never coming back.

And it's the worst feeling in the world.

Through the window of the hearse, I watch Saturday afternoon pass by.

Dad will be in the pub, watching the footie with his mates. Any minute he'll text me to join him for a bit of post-match punditry, then we'll walk, like we always do, up to see the horse, put the world to rights, and I'll tell him everything that's going on. I'll tell him about meeting Oona. How I can't stop thinking about her, how I've fallen under her spell.

Well now, it is the season of the witch.

Then the black cars pull up outside our house, and there are people from the church, and I remember, this is simply a nightmare that refuses to end.

I just want to go, to run for the hills where I can breathe.

'Last bit, bro.' Beth smiles through smudged mascara. 'Ready, Mum?'

Mum nods, wearily. Last bit. The final ritual to get

through, where everyone has a drink and a bite to eat, where they can pay their last respects.

The wake.

What evil genius came up with that idea?

✱

'It's Sam, isn't it?'

Charlie extends his hand. He's tall, with a wide smile.

'I... I just wanted to say, what a great fellow your father was... He...' Charlie sips his wine. 'He was always there for us, always pulling everyone along...'

I nod again, catching Beth's eye as she dutifully talks to Dad's pub mates.

'Well...' Charlie's done his bit, run out of things to say. He twists the empty wine glass in his big hand. I take in his uniform, two white chevrons on his shoulders, birds in flight. Charlie's a corporal.

'Were you out there, with Dad? In Afghanistan?'

That name pokes him in the gut, as if it was the butt of a gun.

'Aye... aye, I was.'

'But you weren't on patrol with him?'

Charlie flinches. He knows where I'm going. We can both see Dad in his truck waving for us to hurry up and climb aboard.

'No...' He licks his lips, perhaps feeling the sand of the desert. 'We were on details that morning. I was... at the town perimeter, when I heard that… that…'

'He'd been blown up,' I say and watch Charlie's friendly face fall. I can see why Dad liked him. Time to relieve him from duty.

'Thank you for coming, Charlie.'

I shake his big warm hand again, and Charlie can't say any more, just nods as I head for Mum, where Dad's brother Patrick has his arm around her. And Granny Mitchell, Dad's mum, reaches her wrinkled hands for me.

'Sammy, dear…'

She creaks from her wheelchair and smiles, but that's all she says, as though saying any more would make her disappear into grey smoke. Patrick puts his other great arm around me. Oh God, please don't. He's so like Dad.

'We're here for a few days…' Patrick's ruddy face looks down at me. 'It would be grand to see you all proper like, once…'

His eyes flick around the room, and I laugh.

'Once we're done with all this?'

Patrick looks at me sheepishly. And then he's not like Dad. He's younger, more shy, but I can see Dad's features. The big nose, the blue eyes.

'I'm sorry, Sheila…'

Mum is trembling so much under Patrick's embrace, I think she's going to shudder into pieces, but somehow she smiles through it.

'Don't be, Patrick. It will be good to see you both.'

She bends down to hear Granny Mitchell better. I

know she means well, and she just wants to connect with her lost son through Mum, but I want her to stop, with her shaking hands, her old wet eyes. I want her to stop filling Mum with more sadness, soaking up everything from this room, these glum people, this moan of mourners. Mum catches my eye.

'Love, would you bring me and Patrick a whisky?' She pinches my chin. 'Your father would be shocked to see his little brother without a glass in his hand.'

Patrick chuckles. 'He'd be doing his nut, Sheila.'

I don't want to go, but that look from Mum tells me I must. I slip into the kitchen, and I'd be lying if I didn't say how blissful it felt to be free of that room.

Afternoon sun from the window slides over glasses and bottles, plates of cellophaned food. I lean against the sink to look at White Horse Hill, arching its great green back towards the sky.

'I thought you would have legged it by now.'

Beth has two empty plates in her hands. 'Is one of those for me?'

'Mum and Patrick…'

'Ah.' Beth sniffs a glass. 'Well, this won't do.' She downs it. 'You need Irish for an Irishman.'

'Oh…'

I can't find the right bottle, my hand is shaking.

'Sam, I can do this – go get some air.' Beth nods towards the hill, the beckoning light. 'I know you're desperate to.'

'I can't. Mum…'

'Mum's in good hands…'

We watch her in the living room. She laughs at something Patrick says. Patrick bringing a bit of Dad back to life.

'Go.' Beth refills the glasses, barging me gently away. 'Before I change my mind.'

I blink at her, my little sis and her bright green eyes full of how she knows, how she nails everything and misses nothing. I wish I had her power.

She kisses my cheek, and for a second rests her head against my mine, transferring her thoughts, uploading her heart, before she sniffs and turns to say,

'Don't forget a certain someone, he's bursting.'

From his basket, Alfie's brown-patched gaze meets mine.

I yank the back door open. I can smell the muck on the fields.

'Give him my love, Sam. Give Dad my love.'

Alfie and I don't need telling again, as behind us the garden gate clatters, singing our escape.

Alfie barks with glee, barking for both of us, and I have to stop climbing, catch my breath, as I turn in the dusky sunlight to gaze down the hill.

Everything stretches beneath me. Our village, with its houses tucked among trees that line the fields, and far away I spy people, little ants on the landscape. Mary, our neighbour, leading her grandchild through her garden. Kids in the playground, laughing down the slide. The park football pitch where a man sits on a bench, a dog by his side. Lads parked up under puffs of smoke.

Alfie barks. There's a stick at my feet.

'All right, then…'

I fling it, high up the hill, towards a tree stump that rears from the gorse, a solitary sentinel.

It's Odin, Sam. King of the gods, waiting to lead the dead.

The stories Dad would tell me and Beth as we walked. How Odin called fallen warriors to join his hunt. And full of his tales, we would head to that stump to play. It was our camp, where we pretended to be Saxon chiefs, and spread our picnic banquet, eating sandwiches and crisps, watching the world that couldn't see us.

A bird swoops.

I shade my eyes. A hawk. No, an owl. It turns its wings, surfing the wind. That sharp curve of its beak as it surveys the earth. Is this what it feels like to be prey? Not daring to move as Death passes over. I glance back at our house. Death's there too, never far away.

Alfie barks, loud and fast. I can't see him.

'Here, boy!'

I whistle.

The sun is falling, bright yellow through the bushes. Again Alfie barks. Sheep shelter in this gorse. If he's trapped one...

'Alfie, come!'

But he doesn't, just barks and barks. I start to run.

'Alf!' He's in the gorse for sure. I crouch and peer in. His scrawny legs scrabble among the shadows.

I stoop under the branches, and a memory flits past, of me and Beth hauling our backpack, gasping and jubilant at our find. The bestest camp ever.

Alfie whines, eyes glinting. He refuses to move

'You're really making me do this...'

The gorse is thick, branches tug like little hands. The wind hums. I push through – Alf's in front of me. He's trembling all over.

'What is it?'

I pull on his collar, but he won't budge.

'Alf… Come… On…'

I squeeze against him, fur one side, brambles the other.

'For flip's sake!' He licks my cheek. 'Let me…' Whining as I push past, and peer into that dark corner.

There's nothing there…

No. There is something. A ball. A white ball.

'What? Scared of a ball now?'

Sunlight dapples, catches its little sparkles, grains of silver.

I reach forward. Alfie barks, leaping into my arm.

'Hey!'

I haul on his collar, but he yelps and jumps like mad, and I see red.

'Alfie! Leave it, will you!'

He stops, panting, his head cocked.

Because it's Dad's voice shouting, and that doesn't make sense because Dad's dead. I don't smell like Dad. It's as if Dad is here in the camp that me and Bethy made, and he's holding Alfie and I can't help it, tears are in my eyes, and I'm crying, snotting in these bushes, while a little dog nuzzles my ear.

'Alfie…' My tears fall. 'I'm sorry…'

He paws me. Gently, I butt him away.

'Now…'

And Dad's close, whispering with me,

Now…

Reaching with me for that strange ball.

Let's see what...

My fingers stretch, close around it. And grab.

We can see...

Ice cold to touch. Not a ball. A stone.

Alfie barks and barks and barks.

'Alf... SHUT...!'

My dad's voice. My dad. My dad.

There's a pounding in my head and I see flashes of light.

A little girl, black hair and white face. She's dancing on the hillside.

Flash.

An older girl, red haired. Freckled and fierce.

Flash.

They're gone and he's there.

Dad.

He smiles at me.

'Dad!'

He turns to the ridge. There's a man. As tall as a tree.

A giant, who opens his one eye, and Dad's words sing through my head.

Odin, King of the gods.
Waiting to lead the dead.
'DAD!'
He shouts, but I can't hear.
I want to run. But I can't move.
Flash.
Flash.
Flash.
'Wait! Dad!'
But he's gone.

I rub my eyes.
The sun is low, blinding through the gorse. Tricks of the light. It must have been…

Alfie whines.

'It's okay, boy…'

I'm tired, that's it. This day has done me in, making me see things. Alf's wet nose nudges my hand, and I feel the weight of the stone. It's heavy.

'Come on, daft dog…'

We crawl out, sharp little goblin hands dragging at us. I look back at our shelter, seeing me and Bethy sharing a coke and a comic, hidden and happy.

The wind has picked up. It's cold, probably getting late. I shudder slightly, and open my fist.

The stone is white, like an egg.

I turn it, catching those grains of silver. There's a notch, as if a fingernail has been pressed in. It sits in my palm so neatly.

'Nice find, Alfie...'

I toss the stone, catching it with a slap against my palm. Alfie jumps.

'It's not a ball, you dodo...'

He barks and pushes at my side, sharp claws digging.

'Ow! Oi!' I hold the stone out of his reach.

Alf flattens to the ground, ears back. He's scared.

'Alf, calm down!'

A bird screams over, so close I can see its yellow eyes, feel the whirl of its wings.

It's the owl.

'Look at that! Thought you were a rabbit, Alf!'

But he only growls, as I point with my hand gripping the stone. And then it's strange. As the owl turns in the sky, I see the stone move. No, it's those silver grains. They're like clouds boiling, like faraway stars.

Alfie barks and the owl cries.

Dad, you would have loved this. Dad. Dad.

I draw the stone to my chest, I'm flying down into those clouds as I think of him. Dad who can't love anything, because he's dead and gone, a ghost in my head.

Now, Sam...

The owl cries again as I draw the stone to my forehead. I don't know why. It feels so cool against my brow.

Let us see, what...

Everything goes white.
We can see...
As I fly into clouds.

I soar, wind cleaving my wings.
The earth turns far below, vast
and green.
And there, I spy a man-boy, his
little dog.
I am bound to him.
From my world to his.
His messenger, his guide.

And I swoop.

I can see it coming. I wrench the stone
from my forehead, as the owl plummets.
White as light. Into me.

I cry out.

I fall.

And fall...

I sit up, searching the orange sky.

Nothing.

But the round white stone lies in the grass next to me. I remember holding it cool against my forehead, seeing clouds and stars.

When I'd looked at that owl I'd flown, the wind lifting me. I'd seen through its eyes.

Alfie sits close.

'I'm losing it, Alf...'

What do people call them? Waking dreams? But it felt so real. Like the stuff I saw in the gorse. Those strange girls. Dad. The giant opening his eye.

I shake my head. Must be dehydrated or something.

Or something.

My phone buzzes and I fumble to find it.

Hey, you okay? Your sis needs you! X

Soz, I text. **Coming x**

I look at the glistening stone.

Tentatively, I reach and prod it with a finger. Alfie's ears prick. I roll it in my palm. But I don't become a bird.

My phone buzzes. A patter of hearts and unicorns.

I'm coming, Bethy, I'm coming...

'How was camp?'

I start, swallowing dry sandwich. Beth stands in the doorway. Everyone's gone.

'All right, I saw an...' Bread clogs my mouth. 'An owl...'

Beth fills the kettle.

'Mum's gone to bed. You were ages, Sam... Could've done with some help here.' She turns to me. 'What's that?'

'What?' I look into her eyes, wide green on alert.

'That...' She touches my head, there's mud on her fingers.

'We were running...' I lie. 'Alf got in my way and...'

'Sammy...' Beth places her black-nailed hand on my face. 'What are you like...?'

'I'm fine, Bethy...'

I move her hand away, keeping it in mine. On her thumb, written in curling white, *'I love you, Dad.'*

'Are you really fine, Sam?'

Her fingers grip mine, not letting go.

'Because I'm...' She gasps for breath. 'I'm... not...'

She's shaking. Quickly I catch her, smother her sobs.

'... ay... as o... it...,' she says into my shoulder, as I rock her reflection in the window.

'What's that, Bethy?' I stroke her head.

'I said...' She takes a breath. 'Today was so shit, but...'

I know what she's going to say by her smile, blinking a black tear.

'Tomorrow's just another day...'

Because Dad sang it. All the time. Our dad who croons in every corner.

Beth yawns, pain passed, out of puff. She slopes from the kitchen, humming Dad's favourite song.

'Night, Bethy.'

She climbs the stairs and *creak, creak, creak* goes the ceiling.

Alfie growls.

'*Shhh...* It's only Beth. Here...'

I tear some of the chicken from the curling sandwiches. As I kneel down to his bowl, something jabs my side.

The stone.

I take it out, carefully, as if I'm handling a creature. It's so cold to touch, almost painful, like holding ice.

'Hey, love...'

Mum stands in the doorway.

'I couldn't sleep.' Her voice is croaky. 'Always the way, when you're shattered.' She goes to the sink and fills a glass.

'Ooh, what's that?'

She goes to touch the stone but I snatch it away, burying it in my pocket.

'It's only an old stone I found.' I feel stupid.

She looks at me and sighs.

'You're not still wanting to go in Monday, are you?'

I keep my hand buried, trapping the stone.

'Yes, Mum, I want to…'

She sighs again.

'Sam, can we talk soon?'

'Okay…'

'About your dad.' She rests her hand on my chest. 'About what happened between you…'

'Oh…' I don't want to talk about that. I pull away from her. 'Here's me thinking it was about college choices.' I bite down, and Mum drops her head.

'I'm sorry, Mum… We can talk another time, okay?'

Her hand traces my cheek briefly in acknowledgement, as she yawns and goes back upstairs. How does she do it? All those people today. All that hushed small talk, the never-ending condolences. She's so immense, so strong. I should have helped her more. Not run off to the hills to find weird stones.

I take the culprit out of my pocket where I'd hidden it.

Why did I do that? But what if she saw stuff too? Got scared. I can't risk that.

Warily, I place the stone on the sideboard. It clinks against the metal sink. Alfie whines in the dark as we both look at this thing in our house, this thing not from here.

'Yeah, Alfie… I know how you feel.'

So we watch while the stone seems to glow, like a little planet waiting for us to visit.

Beth and Mum are at the kitchen table, with steaming tea.

I chew some toast. I need to get out of here.

'So…' Beth clears her throat. 'You hoping to see this new girl today?'

'I only talked to her at a party, Beth…'

My sister sidles up and rests her chin on my shoulder.

'I know, and isn't it nice to meet new people?'

Now I'm thinking about Oona in that garden, stepping into the light, how she smiled at me. And then Chad my handsome best friend ruining things.

'I think Chad likes her.'

'Oh really? Well…' Beth slips her arms around my blazer front. 'You'd better fight for her, then.'

I feel the stone pressed in my pocket and wriggle from Beth's clutch.

'Let him be, Beth. Have a good day, love. We'll talk later, yes?'

'Great being surrounded by females isn't it?' Beth says.

'Yeah.' I step forward, an astronaut from his mothership. 'The best.'

'Give me a call now, if you want to come home.' Mum

straightens my lapel, like she did on my first day at school. 'People will understand.'

'Hey, what's that on your tie?' Beth points, making me look, and flips my nose with her fingers.

'Good one, Bethy.'

At last they let me go, and I feel them watching me all the way to the back gate.

The school bus coughs beneath me as the world passes by.

An old lady pulls her wheelie-bag and her stiff-legged dog.

A jogger pounds along.

A mum texts. Her toddler flings her little shoe.

Around me kids jostle and jeer, phones bleep and buzz.

There's the road sign for 'School' and I remember that tingle in my gut, when I first travelled on this bus, when secondary was strange and scary. Now it's what I need, because nothing's as strange and scary as the stone in my pocket. That makes me see unknown girls, my dead dad, makes me soar like a bird. Or I've gone mad. Either way I can't tell anyone about this. Not yet. Not till I work it out.

The bus barrels over the hill.

I think about the owl. Being an owl.

Alfie barking and barking.

My hand reaches into my pocket.

Where the stone waits.

And those ragged girls are circling, dancing.

I want to go to them.

Because Dad's there.

'Dad!'

The bus grinds gears.

Dad's there. Standing on the pavement.

He's in uniform, camouflaged against the trees, as he steps into the road.

I can see the crow's feet around his blue eyes, the hair on his chin, his smile as he salutes. The bus moves off. I rush to the back window.

'It's Dad! Out of the way!'

He's in the middle of the road, still saluting, still smiling. Cars *beep-beep* and branches slide across the window, as Dad raises a hand to wave.

'Dad! Dad!'

But he's gone. As if he was never there.

I turn around and the entire bus is watching me. Even the phones have stopped.

I feel a flush in my cheeks. Nobody dares laugh, or say a word, because I have Death around me. I might as well be Death.

The bus judders to a stop. A mob of black uniforms charges forward, shouting and shoving and I'm swept along, like a sleepwalker.

But this isn't a dream. I saw Dad. I *know* I saw him.

And then I feel my hand clasped around the stone. It's done it again.

I try to look behind me, above the heads, but there are too many, and somehow I know I won't see him. Somehow it's to do with this thing in my hand.

I turn it, ice cold under my fingers. Somehow.

A football flies up, arcs above the giant shoeboxes of campus. Voices around me grow louder and sharper. Just when I feel I can't take them anymore, when those laughs and shrieks are about to split my head in two, I see her.

She's chatting with some other girls. She laughs and, as I watch, she looks around, searching the crowd, almost as if she can sense me.

And her eyes find mine.

It's like being hit by lightning, boiling my belly into my shoes. She waves, and her mates step away, as she comes towards me, so it's just us. Us and one thousand two hundred pupils and forty-five teaching staff.

'Hey, Sam.'

'Hey, Oona.'

The mob flows, shrieking and pushing. Everyone's feeling it, these precious moments before the bell. Last kicks, texts, vapes, kisses. I think about what it would feel like to kiss Oona's lips.

'What are you reading?' I point at the book sticking out of her bag.

Oona moves it, so I can see the title in curving green letters, *The Diviner's Guide to Dowsing*.

'What's dowsing when it's at home?'

We fall into step, moving through the bodies. I feel such a buzz to be near her. And nervous as anything.

'It's a divining art, Sam.' She tucks her hair behind one perfect ear. 'You use the forked branches of a tree to find water deep underground.'

'You're winding me up!'

I gaze at her. I could do it for the rest of time.

'My mother didn't believe it.' She stops a football neatly, then rolls it back to some year seven kids. She's so unbearably cool, where did she come from? 'Till one day she tried it, and I watched her burn her palms, trying to stop the branches turn...' Oona looks towards the oak tree beyond the playground, its leaves are turning brown. 'That was the day she knew.'

'Knew what?'

A wind picks up, makes the old oak groan, lifts Oona's dark hair across her freckled face. She grins.

'That, like her mother, she had a witching way.'

The oak leaves twist and tumble, dancing in the wind, and I remember two girls laughing, joining their hands in a circle.

'Sam, how... did it go?'

'How did what go?'

'Your dad's...' She flushes and I'm thinking about her lips again. 'Your dad's funeral. I'm sorry...'

'Oh... It was...' But I don't want to think about it. I step closer. 'It was —'

Two lads barge into us, knocking me flat.

'Oi!' I shout as they bundle away.

Oona's above me, saying something, but all I hear is the second bell taunting me.

Time's up, Sam – you should have kissed her when you had the chance!

Then her hand is in mine and she's pulling me into the herd, all mooing into the school shed.

Her hand is soft in the secret of the crowd, and I watch the pink tip of her tongue between that perfect white smile, and heat warms my guts. Being back at school is the best.

'Go raibh an ghaoth go...' I feel her fingers trace my palm, 'brách ag do chúl.'

'Is that Gaelic?' My skin tingles at her touch.

She nods. 'It means, "May the wind be always at your back."'

She laughs and it's the best laugh in the universe. I watch her step away, not wanting her to go, feeling like this is the last time on earth I'll ever see her, with her big eyes watching me, watching me, till finally she's gone, lost in space.

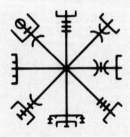

Forty-eight hours since we buried you.

You and Mum walked me to school that very first day.

I was so terrified and excited. My new uniform felt scratchy.

I didn't want to go in, and clung to Mum's legs.

You picked me up and we looked through the classroom window.

We saw all the pictures on the walls.

You took me in and sat, a giant on a tiny chair.

We drew a dinosaur, until we were surrounded by children, all drawing too.

Cats and birds, princesses and super heroes.

I barely felt you gently kiss my head.

I didn't even look up when you left.

Second bell blasts out. I spot Darren and Ben sniggering over their phones, Chloe and Tash scandalously wide-eyed with *she never did* and *she did, I tell you*. Sharkey spies me through his long hair and raises a thumb. Then Chad is sliding into the seat next to me.

'Hey.' He nudges me.

'Hey.' I nudge him back.

'Why haven't you—'

'All righty, everyone! Phones down or they're history.'

Mr Chandler surveys the class. Chad puts down his phone and pulls out a pad to write. I know what it will say.

'Let's smash this registration, shall we?'

There's a groan at Mr Chandler's 'youth speak'. He grins through his hipster beard. We call him Carlito after that Al Pacino film. Chad pushes his pad over. It reads,

Why haven't you returned my texts?

As Carlito calls out names, waiting for the 'here, sir', I write,

Burying Dad.

I bite my lip. I can't help myself. Chad writes fast,

I know, mate. I'm sorry. I'm here for you, is all.

'Charlie Harding!'

'Here, sir!' Chad calls.

That's nice.

I can feel him looking at me, but I don't look at him.

'Sam Mitchell!'

'Here, sir!'

Chad's phone buzzes. **1 message from Oona Fitzgerald.**

He swipes his phone off the desk. Now I do look at him.

'Harding, I mean it, that phone will be dust!'

'Sorry, sir,' Chad mumbles and glances at me with a slight smile.

'Chloe Simms!'

'Here!'

And perhaps it's just for weird comfort, but my hand drifts to my pocket as I write in caps,

BASTARD.

'Gina Williams!'

'Here, Mr Chandler, sir!'

Now it's Chad's turn to stare at me.

'What's wrong with you?' he hisses.

My hand closes around the stone, as I write,

You.

'What do you mean, mate?'

'Mate? Ha!'

The laugh barks out of me. I feel my lip quiver.

'What's going on?' Mr Chandler's in front of our table. The class has turned to watch us.

'What are you all looking at?' My grip tightens.

'Sam...'

'I'm... I'm surprised to see you, Sam.' Mr Chandler squats. 'How are you?'

How am I? I stare at my reflection in Carlito's big square lenses. My spirit self, trapped in glass.

'Oi, wake up—' Chad tugs me round.

'Get off me!'

'Whoa, Sam – calm down.'

'I am calm!' My hand is a fist of stone.

'Sam,' Mr Chandler touches my shoulder, 'I'm really not sure you should be here...'

'I SAID, I'M OKAY!' My voice bites the air.

And in a bound I jump the table, sending chairs flying.

'Sam!' Chad shouts.

But I'm bounding through the class, my legs are springs.

'Sam, I didn't mean...'

I tear through the doorway, growling for everyone to clear off. I catch their startled expressions as I pass. Chloe and Gina all *omg*. Darren pointing. Sharkey filming. And I laugh at them as they reel away.

'Did he bite you, sir?'

'Sit down. Sam! Come back!'

But I'm not coming back, as I race along the corridor, turn tail, and skid around the corner.

Thump, bump goes the stone in my blazer.

I know where to go. Where I can sit and think.

So I run and run and run.

The library doors hush behind me.

I stop, panting, breathing in the books, their musty papery smell. What happened back there was a blur. **1 message from Oona Fitzgerald.**

Does she like him? She must. The whole world fancies Chad.

In the hall the bell sounds.

Second period. Got time to think. Need to work out this mad thing in my pocket. I don't dare take it out.

'Hello, Sam,' Mrs Pratt, the librarian, acknowledges me from her desk.

I like Mrs Pratt. She won't dob me in. I'm in her library, so that's good enough for her.

'Oh... That book you were asking about came in. Remember?' She rattles into her PC. 'You were ever so keen to reserve it before...' She stops punching keys. 'Before...'

'I was off school,' I save her.

'Yes.' She nods, a flash of silver in her smile. 'Ah, here

we are...' She taps her screen. *'Gods of the Underworld: Deities of the Dark.'*

I tumble back through a hundred years. I'd ordered that book because Dad would be home soon. Because I knew he'd love it. Because we could talk about it as we climbed the hill to see the White Horse. But we never did.

Mrs Pratt hands me a slip of paper.

'It's there, between History and Geography.'

I study the slip, her careful pencil marks.

'Thanks, Mrs Pratt.' I smile. 'I'll find it.'

And I make for the aisles, those tunnels of books, as she calls after me,

'Let me know what it's like!'

I step between the long shelves and shake thoughts of Dad away. I'm alone in the labyrinth and I know my way, passing books on the local region, histories, legends and maps. I've browsed here so many times, digging for gold. *The Folklore of the West, Prehistoric Monuments, The Old Gods.* I've stood for ages reading under the flickering strip lights. Even the day after Dad died, I was here, watching my tears pitter-patter onto pages.

I check Mrs Pratt's note. I'm close. My hands skim across spines, gently, as if they're slumbering. Then I see it. Its fresh binding proud of the older volumes. I ease it from the shelf.

The title is a swirl of gold, edged with a pattern of symbols.

'Cuneiform,' I whisper, savouring that word,

remembering what Dad had told me.

It's the oldest known writing, Sammy.

I start, getting that hairs-on-the-neck thing when you think you're alone, and then realise you're not. But there's nothing. Just rows of sleeping books.

Pages flick under my fingers, bright desert, green hills, ruins of tombs, ancient statues, jewelled hoards. And so many strange names. The Morrigan, Hades, Yama.

I stop at a picture. The side-on figure of a man with a wolf's head.

Anubis, the Egyptian god of the dead who ushered souls into the afterlife...

Against the shelf, I can feel the stone in my pocket.

That wolf's head, its staring eye.

I turn the page. And my heart skips. I've seen this picture before. From the book Dad gave me all those years ago. It's an engraving of a huge bearded man, with one eye, under a wide-brimmed hat. At his feet sit two huge wolves, and nesting on his shoulders, two frowning ravens.

Odin, the Norse king of the gods.

... the watcher of the dead, stories told of him striding the land... wise, magical, able to shift his shape, the god of the wild hunt, leading fallen warriors on a gallop across the sky.

A wind whistles through my memory. Of that day, walking with Dad. When we saw him.

The tall man high on the hill, his long hair flying.

Odin in the picture raises his staff. Like that man did then, hailing us.

While huge shapes loped behind him.

He's got big dogs, hasn't he?... Must be an animal trainer or something.

Not Alsatians, Dad.

Wolves.

Shall we wave, Sam? Maybe he'll bring us luck.

But I couldn't, instead I just watched you, waving at the man in the wind, the watcher of the dead.

I feel hot and shake my head. Something moves in the corner of my eye.

I look up, expecting to see Mrs Pratt. But it's not Mrs Pratt.

A man is leaning against the shelves, his back to me as he reads.

I can hear him whistling softly. A tune I know.

'Tomorrow's just another day...'

He's in uniform. Like. Like.

'Dad?'

He closes the book and walks into the shadow.

'Dad!'

I run to catch him, as he rounds a corner.

But he's gone.

The aisle is empty.

The book is still open in my hand.

... the god of the wild hunt, leading fallen warriors.

What if we had walked up to that tall figure, would he

have towered above us as he summoned his birds?

Dad! Look!

Would we have heard the croon of a raven in his nest of hair?

Well, I'll be...

Would he have gazed at us, a leather patch over one eye?

He is waving, Dad!

Would he have reached up to slowly fold it back?

Go on, then, say hello!

To show his eye, completely white. Like the stone in my pocket.

Growing brighter and brighter.

Splitting my head.

Sending me into oblivion.

I was twelve when he first went.

'Sam? That you?'

Mum's voice from the kitchen. No way I could sneak up the stairs now. I put my football on top of the scattered letters and see myself in the hall mirror. There's mud above my eye.

'Sam?'

'Yeah.' No escape. Why didn't I stay away? But I know why. Mum would have never forgiven me.

'Please come
in here, love. I told you to be
back at three. We've not got long now...'

I stomp towards the kitchen, not bothering to kick
off my boots. My little rebellion.

The kitchen door's open. I can hear them murmuring
as I put my hand on the handle.

'Hey now, Bethy... Hey now... don't be like that...'

Beth sniffs, and I know she's got her head buried in
Dad's shoulder.

'And while I'm gone, your brother will be here for
you...'

I feel that pain in my throat. The one that comes from
when you really want to cry, but you're trying to stop it.
And that makes you want to cry even more. I push the
door open.

'And here he is now, see... here's your big brother.'

When Dad whispers his Irish accent gets all the more
Irish. He looks at me. And he winks. Of course he winks.

'How was the game, son?'

'Two–one. To us,' I cough through that hand crushing
my throat.

'That's grand – and did you score?'

I nod. Because I think if I speak again and I see all
that pride glisten in his eyes, I know I'll start to cry, and
I won't, I can't.

'Well done, love...' Mum dabs the mud from my

temple. Her smile is thin, as though someone's drawn it on with a hard pencil.

'Beth thinks I'm not coming back, Sammy.' Dad strokes my sister's head. 'You don't think that, do you?'

I look at the smile in his blue eyes. The dimples in his cheeks. I look at the camouflage of his uniform, useless in our bright kitchen. I look at his kit bag resting against the fridge, and a drawing there by Beth of us all, colourful stick figures dancing around the White Horse.

'Sam, love?'

'Where is it, again…' I force the words through the ache, 'that you're going, Dad?'

His eyes look straight into mine. He's willing me to be strong.

'Afghanistan,' he says. That name. It should sound mysterious. But it just means Dad is gone.

'I thought we won the war.'

'Wars are easy to start, son, not so easy to end…'

Beth's head shakes again, her arms tighter than tight around Dad's neck.

Mum reaches for me, but I don't move. My feet are bags of cement.

'Sammy, it will pass quickly. Your dad's tour will be over and—'

'But we don't know, do we?' I blurt out.

They both look at me. Mum and Dad. Holding themselves together for us. But I don't want them to. I want them to shout and cry. I want them to be angry, that there's this bloody war on, that my dad is a soldier, that he might die.

'We don't know if Dad will come back, do we?'

Beth turns her head. There's snot on Dad's shoulder.

'Don't say that!'

Her eyes blaze green at me. But I can't help myself. I can't stop.

'Beth, I'm agreeing with you – you just said it yoursel—'

'Take it back!'

'But we don't, Beth!'

'Take it back, Sam!'

'Kids, please don't fight…' Dad draws us both to him.

'I don't want to leave you in a row, now do I?'

'Alan, they'll be calling for you soon…'

'Aye, okay…'

My parents' voices are muffled through Dad's big arms around us.

'Here – here now before I go… Look, Beth.'

He pulls back and reaches into his kit bag.

'I found her – up near the White Horse. Right next to her mum…'

A little white foal cuddly toy trots over his knee, and Beth smiles to reach for it, as it neighs and nuzzles her nose.

'There now – you keep her safe till I get back, you hear?'

She nods, full of love for him, for the glassy eyes of her foal.

'And, Sammy, what do I have here for you, eh?'

I watch him reach into his kit bag. He's like army Santa rootling around to pull out his gift. It's a book. There's a silver dragon on the front.

'Promise you'll lend it to me when you're done?' Dad smiles.

I turn the pages, smelling the fresh wood through a blur of pictures.

'Norse Myths and Legends...' Mum says. 'Well now, that'll keep you quiet for a while, won't it?' She brushes my hair from my eyes, and as she does, I hear, we all hear, the sound of a van drawing up outside.

'See, Sam – here's the fella I was telling you about...' Dad turns the pages, leaning into me. I don't want him to leave. I want him to stay and tell me stories. I want him to walk with me up to the White Horse, where we can sit and watch the endless world below us, where there's no war, only red kites and clouds. I blink through a mist of tears.

'See... isn't this a fine picture?'

His hand on my back, he traces a picture of a tall bearded man. There's a patch across his eye. Two wolves from his side look out at me, and two ravens squint from his shoulders.

'Odin...' he reads. 'A god who walked the vale with his wild hunt, leading the dead to his hall...'

'Is he your favourite god, Daddy?'

Dad laughs, pinching Beth's cheek.

'I suppose he is…' He laughs again. 'My favourite god. What do you think, Sam?'

A horn sounds.

'Come here, all of you…'

And Dad suddenly has hold of us all, wrapping us close, as Odin looks at us over his shoulder, wolves poised to pounce, ravens ready to fly.

'Be good, look after each other…'

We watch as Dad swings up, taking his smile away, tucking it into his camouflage jacket and beret, becoming a soldier standing in our kitchen.

The horn sounds again. Longer.

'Sheila…'

We watch as he kisses Mum.

'Don't see me to the door now… Because I…'

He swallows, searching for words as he swings his kit bag over his shoulder. 'I'll be back before you know it.'

Like he's popping to the shops, or going to the pub. With one last look at Mum, he walks away and we watch until he's gone.

I open my eyes.

Cork panels on a ceiling, steel tracks and wires.

I raise my head. It hurts so much. Taste in my mouth, like metal.

I look around. A hospital ward.

Cautiously, I feel my head. Scratchy strips are glued along my temple. I press lightly and pain throbs back.

My stuff is folded on a chair. And now I see I'm in a – I don't know what – a long blouse or something. A jug of water sits on a tall table. A *beep beep* sounds from somewhere. Hospital bits around me – a light on a pivot arm, a pull cord, and a white board. In black marker I can see scrawled:

Mitchell, Sam. Head injury, poss. concussion.

Concussion.

I remember. The library. Wolves. A burning light. And I fell. I remember, I fell, because the last thing I heard was the sound of the—

Stone.

Quickly, I reach for my stuff. Trousers, pants and socks, my shirt and tie. But not my blazer. Where's my blazer?

They wouldn't have taken it, would they? I swivel the chair round.

Through pain and panic, I see my blazer over the armchair. The pocket swings heavily. I feel the hard, round weight of it. I feel sick and sweaty.

My hand shakes as I reach for the water.

A nurse bustles over, her heels squeaking. She pushes a little cart that rattles to a stop.

'Hi, Sam, how are you feeling? Do you have any pain?' She smooths my bed. Her name clip says 'Faith Massani'.

'Yus… My head.' My words clog up.

Her eyes flick across my temple.

'You had quite a bump. I'll bring you something…'

'Wait. When's…? I mean, how long…? What time…?' It's as though I'm talking through glue.

Faith watches me calmly, but not me. She's looking at a patient who's got butterfly stitches on his bonce and is rambling like a zombie.

'You've been here since ten this morning. It's… three thirty now.' She turns, then tuts. 'Oh, your mother and sister went to grab a tea, and – ah, here they are!'

Faith moves off, smiling at Mum and Beth.

'Sam!' Beth runs forward. 'You're awake!'

They've been crying. Seeing them here in this strange

setting, I want to cry too. I feel about five. I want them here, but I don't want them here, don't want fuss. But I am here, and it's my fault they're here.

'Mum, I'm all right.' Her face is smiling, but tense. I did that. 'Don't wuzzy…' They look at each and back at me. 'Honestly… I'm fine, it was just a bung… I mean, a…'

'Sam, rest up.' Beth grins. Her hand is hot from holding the tea. 'Besides, it's too funny.'

Mum strokes the side of my face that isn't throbbing. She looks better than… when was the funeral? Yesterday? Today? I feel like a broken clock.

'So, how are we all doing?'

Faith's back. She has a little cup and some water.

'For your pain, young man.' She hands me the cup. 'It will make you drowsy. But you're allowed to sleep, now you've woken up.'

That doesn't make much sense. But then nothing does at the moment.

I neck the pill, feeling their eyes on me.

'He must rest, Mrs Mitchell.' Faith takes the cup from me.

I close my eyes. So tired suddenly.

'Can we stay with him?'

'Of course, of course…' Fingers on my wrist, finding my pulse, the beat of my heart. So very tired. I'm tumbling down a deep dark well.

Like a stone falling, falling. White in the blackness.

'He's nodding off, Mum.'

I see him, in the aisle, his camouflaged back to me.

'Beth, what are we going to do? I shouldn't... I shouldn't have let him go in.'

'It's not your fault, Mum.'

'Oh my Sammy, my Sam...'

'Where are you?'

'We're here, Sam. We're here.'

'The doctors have given me the name of someone, Beth. Who can speak to him?'

'If he'll speak to them...'

'We have to try, Beth. He won't let me in. Not since...'

Dad's hand is warm on my neck. Wind tugs the grass as we walk. The White Horse gallops on, carved into the hill, ever leaping through time.

'I love this place, Sam. I want to be here for ever.'

'The horse is so old, isn't it, Dad?'

'Oh yeah, older than me even. Here, look at this...'

I look, and see in his palm something white and round, little speckles of brown.

'Shell from an owl. For you.'

'Ah, I love it.'

'I love you, son. More than salt.'

'Salt...'

'He's hallucinating. The school said he was lashing out, shouting about wolves. Oh God, I'm so worried for him, Beth.'

The man strides along the ridge where ravens reel and cry.
'Who's that, Dad?'
His shape is getting smaller, sinking beyond the hill vanishing in the light.

'I know, Mum. I know...'

I hear the sound of pages turning, birds tweeting.

I'm under the tree in the garden with Beth, our bikes close by, ready for a race to the river. Beth's been trying to beat me all summer. Eventually she will, of course, with a warrior queen cry.

I turn my head, through pulsing pain.

We're not in our garden. That curtain rail isn't the circling branch of our tree. Our bikes aren't leaning against my hospital bed, the birds are the *bleep bleep*s of the ward.

But Beth's real. She's reading when her phone buzzes. I watch her eyes sparkle as she texts back.

Bleep. Bleep.

My head crackles as I sit up, swing my legs out.

'Hey, what's up?' Beth starts. 'Need the loo?'

'Y-yeah.' I grab for my clothes. 'Can you help?'

'Sure, but you won't need…'

'Where… Where you get that?'

The book she's holding. It's the one from the library. My head throbs with that white searing light.

'They found it when… Mrs Pratt checked it out for you.' She opens it to the picture of Odin. 'I remember Dad's stories about this guy wandering the hills. I always liked his wolves. They don't seem scary somehow…' Her black witchy fingernail strokes a wolf's head from top to tail. I can hear its panting.

'Where's Mum?' I pull on trousers, blazer, moving quickly.

'She's meeting with Dr Fellowes.'

'Who?' I spot Faith at the front desk, bent over her work. I check my phone. A text from Chad.

Got Dad's keys to the Beast! Just arrived at hospital to see you.

'She's a psychothera—' Beth grabs me. 'Wait, you don't need the loo, do you?'

I feel cold suddenly and huddle into my blazer, the stone jabs my hip, keen to be going, somewhere, anywhere.

'I need some air.'

'You're concussed, Sam. And you're shivering.'

'I'm fine.' My head bangs like several hammers.

'Young man, what's all this, now – we can't have you wandering about.'

Faith is looking at me, and round the desk comes another nurse. My hand steals into my pocket.

'I'm sorry.' Beth's hooking her arm in mine. 'I'll get him back.'

'Hey, laddy, the doc's not discharged you yet,' the male nurse tells me.

'I thought he needed the loo—'

'No bother, lassie…'

I stroke the shape of the stone.

'… let me help you along there, Sam.'

'No.' I feel a growl rise in me.

'Hey, now…'

He reaches, and I push back, my chest swelling. I see him stare.

'What the…?'

'Sam!'

'Shall I call security?' Faith reaches for her phone.

He tries to push my steely body, his feet slip as I move.

'Sam, what's going on?'

I grab her hand. And run.

'Sam! Stop!' screams Beth.

She trips, panting like a pup.

'Sam, I can't…'

Swiftly, I lift her and bound on.

Light and shouting and faces. I roar through them, twisting and turning.

'Sam!' she cries. 'Sam, put me down! Sam, please!'

I stop. She's frightened of me.

I look about.

'Sam, what is going on?'

I feel my phone buzz.

'I'm sorry, Bethy, I had to get out of there.'

Wisps of dark hair blow across her green glare.

'What happened back there? That nurse couldn't hold you. And you lifted me like that? Are you…?' Her voice drops. 'Are you on something?'

'No! 'Course not!' I feel the guilty weight of the stone. But I can't tell her. I'm too scared of what it is. And then I see it. That beaten-up old army Land Rover, the Beast waiting in all its khaki glory.

'Then how did—?'

But I'm already moving. I'm sorry, Bethy. I need to get away. Even from you.

Chad waves. He's wearing a stupid pair of mirrored aviators.

'Woah, look at the state of y— Oh, hi, Beth…'

I watch him flush as Beth stands in a fury of folded arms.

'Oh, hi, Chad, what a surprise. Come to help, have you?'

'Y-yeah…' He flushes harder, looking from me to Beth. 'Can I… Can I give you a lift?'

'Not on a provisional licence, you can't!' shouts Beth behind me. 'If you have an accident —'

'I won't. I'm a careful driver.' Chad looks so dumb in those shades.

'An illegal driver. Sam, don't do this.'

'Do what?'

'You're not right – you know you're not!'

'Bethy, I'll be home later – I just need—'

'Oh, YOU! YOU need! Because this is all about YOU, isn't it?'

I mouth words that do not come.

'Great. Well, here's your precious book.' She slams it into my belly, and stalks away, black hair whipping.

'Beth!' I shout at her back, laughing that false laugh when you're hiding something. 'Beth!'

'Oh, flipping heck.' Chad watches her go. 'I didn't know Beth… your sister… was here.'

'Why do you care?'

He shrugs. 'Just… not good to upset the women folk, is it? They keep the world turning.' He looks at Beth striding off, then smiles that narrow, handsome smile of his. Chad, ever the charmer.

'Come on, then, Frankenstein, if you're coming.'

I want to correct him, Frankenstein's monster, but my head aches too much, so I climb into the old Land Rover. It smells of stale earth, oil and wood. Chad whacks up the stereo. Old-school hip hop fills the cabin.

'Welcome to the Beast, my friend.' He turns the ignition and the engine revs. 'Where to, then?'

I look at my horror show face in the rear-view mirror.

'Anywhere.' I grin against the pain. 'Provisionally speaking.'

He swings the car around, flooring it, and I grapple for the seatbelt.

Then Chad and me and the Beast roar into the road.

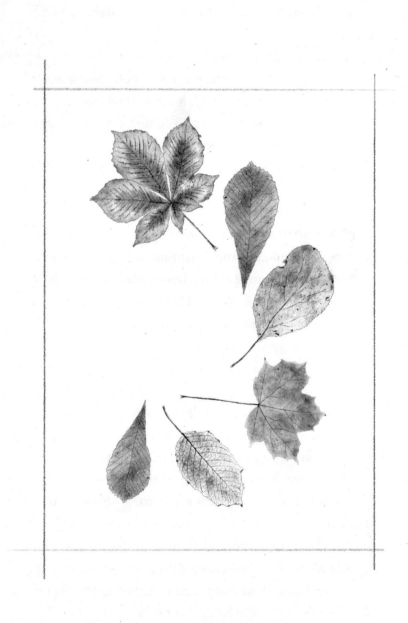

'So what happened, Sam?'

Chad guns the Beast forward, his arm resting on the open window. Leaves swirl in our wake, spirals of yellow and orange. Dad's favourite time of the year.

'Just fell…'

I shake my head and wish I hadn't, the pain makes me wince.

'Heard that one before. Should see the other bloke, right?'

Shops and people pass in a blur. Some kids on bikes salute as we fly past. Chad laughs leaning into a roundabout, where the traffic seems to bow to let us pass. How does he do it? He's so sure of himself. People just want to be around him.

Ahead, the hills bend towards the sky, afternoon light trickling down. What happened in the library? It felt so real. Would anyone believe me if I told them?

We lurch to a stop at some lights and my phone buzzes.
Beth told me you're in hospital?! Hope you're okay.
Thinking of you. X

I stare at Oona's message. Especially that big X. And now I'm thinking about her lips again.

'And we're off!'

Chad howls. I remember Oona's name on his phone. Calling him a bastard. His face, all innocent surprise, what me? Not this time, Chad. We're going to talk, whether he likes it or not.

'So where are we going, then?'

'The Beast says...' he slaps the wheel, 'it's a beautiful day for a bit of off-roading.'

I look out of the window at the hills, green giants beckoning.

'You'll be all right, you've already been in the wars!'

He swerves off the main road, racing through the lanes. Then, just as quickly, brakes hard in the dust. An open gate beckons.

Race you to the top, Sam.

It's as if Dad's sitting behind me, but there's nothing, only the flapping canopy window.

'Don't worry your battered head, Sammy.' Chad revs the engine. 'I've got you!'

We wheel spin forward.

'Here we go!'

He crunches the gears as we roll onto the plain, climbing furrows fast. My body jolts as we bump and I laugh like a kid, my stomach left hanging in the air.

'Hold onto your lunch, amigo!'

The Beast claws earth as we climb and climb and climb, the clear blue sky filling the windscreen. And just when it seems we'll fly, soaring off the edge, we reach the top, wheeling furiously and the world stretches out everywhere, a hopscotch of field upon field.

Chad throws the Beast into a skid, cutting the ignition and cranking the handbrake. We stare at the landscape for a second, letting it right itself. A couple of gulls turn on the wind, spying this strange intruder.

'Come on, then.' Chad swings open his door. 'The view's amazing from up here.'

I step out and the wind tugs at me. Far below us, a tractor beetles along and I follow the ridge of the hills until I see it, a flick of chalk, the tail of the White Horse. And I feel Dad's stubble as he whispers in my ear.

The horse was made to be seen from far away, or from up high.

So much has happened. So quickly and painfully, I can barely catch my breath. The funeral. Finding the stone. Seeing him from the bus. Wolves in the library. Hospital. Perhaps none of it is really happening? Perhaps I died instead of him. I don't know. I don't care. I'm lost. Because the only person I want talk to about what's going on, or not going on, is you, my dear, departed, dead dad.

'That Halloween rave's soon, buddy.' Chad slumps against the creaking Beast and pulls at grass. 'Up at the

White Horse. Should be good, eh?'

Should be good when he turns up with Oona on his arm.

'Mate, what's going on with you?'

Classic Chad pre-emptive strike. Well, I'll outflank him.

'Like you need to ask.'

He takes his shades off, reaches for me. 'Sam, I loved your dad, and I'm always, always here for you about that, but this is something else. That day in class you were so angry. And you've been off with me since the party.'

The party. Oona landing in my life, beamed down from the stars.

'All right, then.' I hold his gaze. 'Why are you messaging Oona Fitzgerald?'

Chad stares. Got him.

'I'm not... I mean...'

His mouth moves, but not even lies come out.

'I saw her name on your phone, Chad.'

'Sam, it's not—'

'You knew I liked her at the party.'

''Course, so I wouldn't —'

'I thought you and Chloe had a thing.'

'Not for ages. Sam —' Chad reaches for me again, 'I don't like Oona like that! And I'm pretty sure she wouldn't be interested in me, even I did, okay?'

'So why's she messaging you?'

He pulls a face. 'She's... she's helping me.'

I laugh and shake him off.

'You're such a liar.'

I turn back to the hills, so real and true. Unlike my so-called friend now on his feet.

'Sam, I'm telling you the truth. Listen to me!'

I round on him, anger making me snarl.

'All right, let's hear it.'

The seagulls laugh. This should be good.

Chad swallows. 'It's somebody else I like. Oona's helping me talk to her.'

His eyes don't leave mine. Is this for real?

'Who?'

'I can't tell you... not yet.'

'Why not?' He shakes his head. 'Why *not*, Chad?'

But as he turns, I see his face. He's not defensive, or angry. Worry floods him.

'Because I don't want to mess it up.' He pulls each word out. 'She means too much.'

Wow. He's never said that about a girl before.

'Ask Oona, if you don't believe me.' He pauses, cocking his head attentively. 'You ask her, all right?'

He eyes me fiercely, ready for more. He means it. And I feel like kicking my heels, howling at this beautiful day. He means it. Oona and Chad aren't a thing.

So I jump for him, folding my arm around his head and laugh. I tousle his lovely locks that send all the girls wild. 'You secret softy!'

'Get off!' He grins, and I can see the relief in him.

'Come on, let's get you back – or that sister of yours will have my guts.'

So we clamber back into the Beast, and Chad chugs us down the hill, with the sun on our necks. How I've missed my friend, even when he's wearing stupid shades.

'Home safe and sound.' Chad hauls on the handbrake, as I clamber out. 'Told you it would be all right. The Beast is never wrong.' He looks over the top of his glasses. 'Looks like you've had company.'

I turn to see Oona and Beth at our front door. My stomach flips.

'I'd better scoot, buddy, before Dad gets back.' Chad doesn't want another Beth drubbing, but my sister is only smiling and nodding to Oona. 'Good luck!' He releases the Beast into the road, and they're gone in a cloud of dust, as if Chad's some cowboy making his escape from the law.

'You certainly know how to wind your sister up, Sam.'

Oona's at our garden gate. There's a bag over her shoulder. Her smile freezes.

'Oh my...' and before I know it, her hand, her beautiful, warm hand is on my cheek, as her dark eyes roam the bump on my head. Not all bumps are bad, it seems.

'Mrs Pratt sends her best.' Her hand moves away, and I fight to not grab it back. 'She doesn't usually have young men fainting in her library.'

The library. I think about Odin's white gaze from the book. A book I fell into.

'Did you… did you come to see me?'

She raises a paint-stroke eyebrow.

'Surely you're not the only person in my life!' She smiles. 'No, I've been doing a reading for Beth.'

'A reading of what?'

I watch as her long hair falls across her bag, and she brings out a pack of cards. There are brightly drawn figures beneath the words 'Tarot. The Guiding Spirit'.

'I didn't know Beth was into stuff like that…'

Oona leans forward and presses my arm.

'"Stuff like that" is as old as the hills, Sam.' Her eyes glint with sharp light.

'Take care of that head, you hear?' Oona's past me, I didn't see her move, as if she ghosted through my body. 'If you play your cards right…' she taps the pack and winks, and my stomach flips again, 'maybe I'll do your reading one of these days.'

'I'd like…'

'Sam!' Beth's watching us from the front door. 'Dinner!'

And when I turn back, Oona's gone, leaving the feel of her hand on my skin.

'Where's Mum?'

Beth lays the kitchen table. Alfie's tail thumps the floor. At least someone's pleased to see me.

'Hurrying back from her shift to see her son.'

My sister pushes me out of the way, dropping a place mat down.

I gulp from a water glass, swilling the guilt. I needed that break with Chad, needed to get onto the plain and breathe. But I know I'm worrying them. I need to make peace.

'So tarot, eh?' I watch Beth stir something in a pot. 'Going to meet any tall, dark strangers?'

'Who's to say I haven't already met them?'

She tastes with a spoon, and finally looks over at me, green gaze beneath her fringe.

I swig again, like a gambler about to play.

'Bethy, I'm so—'

'Save it.' She turns up the heat, and I can only watch her back. 'You can do all your apologies when Mum's back.'

I sigh. There's no winning with Beth when she's like this.

'Seriously, Beth. I'm interested – did Oona help?'

She stiffens. She's not stirring anymore.

'It was… about you and me, I think.'

'Oh?'

'The journeys we're on…' Beth looks up through the window, and I stand slowly. 'How we're on paths that sometimes touch, sometimes don't…' I can hear the waver in her voice, 'and how I… how I…'

I'm at her shoulder, turning her to me as she shakes.

'I have to fight, to not lose you. Lose you too.'

'You're not going to lose me, Bethy. Not never.'

'I will fight, Sam. I'll fight for ever.'

'Me too, Bethy. Me too.'

I hold her and hold her, and we say nothing more till Mum's key turns in the lock.

O · THE FOOL

The letter from the police came a few days later.

We'd been caught on a red-light cam.

Sorry, mate. You were right.

He sent me a photo of the 'Notice of Intended Prosecution', and there's a grainy pic of the Beast and our silly faces. There's me freeze-framed telling him the Beast was too far over the white 'Stop' sign.

Got to sign a caution statement. Lucky Dad was out when this came, he can't find out, Sam...

Mum'll help. I need to tell her... I text back. The police. I feel sick suddenly.

Okay. See you there.

I wait for emojis that don't appear this time. Even Chad knows this is serious.

And with the sick feeling rising, I start to message Mum.

'I put them in Two, Sarge.'

'Much obliged, Ivana.'

The sergeant places one big bear's paw on my shoulder and the other on Chad's, guides us towards a door with a mesh window, and swings it open. Mum and Beth are sitting at a table with plastic cups of tea. They both stand, wide-eyed with relief.

'Sammy…'

Mum darts forward.

'Mum…'

'It's all right, love, it's all right, you're okay, you're okay…' She's whispering and kissing me as I feel Beth's arms pull us close.

'You stupid idiot…' Her voice cracks. 'I warned you.'

'I know, I know…' is all I can say over and over, feeling ashamed and relieved. 'I thought it would be all right. I thought…'

Beth glares at Chad, who looks at the floor.

'Now then, folks, if I could ask you to sit, we can get this over…'

Dutifully, we sit at the grey table, Beth and Mum either side of me. The sergeant prods a form with a chewed nail.

'We've taken a statement from young Chad here – who…' the sergeant lifts Chad's licence, 'who, aside from his red-light offence, we now know was the illegal driver of the vehicle.' Chad's leg jiggles up and down. I watch as Beth reaches to still it. 'So can you confirm this is your own statement, Sam – the one we went through earlier?'

I look at the paper, recognising the sergeant's neat handwriting and I nod.

The policeman stifles a yawn. 'Sign and date here, please.'

I take the pen and write my name, shakily. They're all watching me, and it feels as if the room is holding its breath. The sergeant checks the form.

'That all seems in order...'

'Does...' I shake. 'Does that mean we're free to go?'

He sighs and caps his pen.

'Boys, I had a lad in here last week caught doing one hundred and fifty on the dual carriageway.'

He folds the paper, smoothing it neatly.

'A few days before that we caught another couple swimming in the local weir – beneath the "Risk of Death" sign.'

He slides one of his paws over his short hair. Sergeant Bear.

'And last month's lunatic climbed so far up an electricity pylon they couldn't get down.' He looks steadily at Beth. 'All teenage lads, mind.' Then straight at me and Chad.

'Before you go, think about it: what could be more downright dangerous than you two larking about in a vehicle you're not licensed to drive, not on Her Majesty's highways or anywhere else?'

I feel Beth's hand grip mine, as the sergeant leans forward.

'We don't do three strikes in this neck of the woods,

boys…' He holds up the form. 'This is your card marked. With a capital "C" for caution. As well as a fine and points for young Chad here. Do you understand?'

'Y-yes…' Chad and I can barely get the words out.

'Next time you do something so stupid, you'll be charged. Or, in my infinite experience… you'll both be dead.' That word, ever at my tail. 'Do you understand that too?'

'Yes, sir.' Chad coughs, and for a moment I think he's going to vomit. He's so white.

I lick my trembling lip. 'Yes.' And like a private in his parade, add, 'Sergeant.'

'It's a caution this time because I hear from your mum and sister that you've been going through a lot of stuff, Sam. The hardest stuff.'

It's Mum's turn to grip my hand.

'I am sorry to hear that.' His growl softens. 'But it's good your mum's got you to see someone.'

I don't know what he means.

'We see a few referrals her way. She'll see you right, son.'

'Thank you so much for everything.' Mum's picking up her bag, tugging me and Chad to our feet.

'What referrals?'

Beth's the other side of us and the sergeant is holding the door open.

He calls out, 'Could you buzz these folks through, Ivana, please?'

'Mum?'

Beth and Mum are leading us towards the station door.

'Sam, it's nothing to worry about…'

The main door buzzes and Beth hauls it open, pushing Chad ahead of her.

'I won't say, see you again, lads,' the sergeant says from the desk. 'But do take care of yourselves, for your families' sake, if not yours, eh?' And we're out of the door. Free.

'Mum, see who? What's he talking about?!'

'Sam.' Mum rounds on me, her fingers pressing. 'Calm down, love.'

'But —'

'Beth and I are finding it just as tough…'

'I… I know.' I'm shaking now and so's Mum. I can see the worry scored into her face, making her look old and tired. 'I'm sorry, I just…'

I feel the stone swinging in my pocket, as if it wants to be part of this conversation.

'I just feel a bit strange at the moment, Mum.'

She strokes my face, looking at my bump, the bindings.

'I know, love, I know… That's why I want to help you. With this specialist.'

'But I'm… I'm fine.' The lie makes me smile and Beth's eyes are filling with tears again. I'm so sick of crying.

'For me, love.' Mum's hand is cold on my cheek. 'Do it for me.'

'And me,' says Beth, and they close around me, a huddle against the autumn chill. 'Got you,' she whispers in a creepy voice.

It's what Dad used to say, running to catch us when we were little. A monster after our shrieks.

'I'll eat you up!'

'All right.' I give in, I'm surrounded. 'I'll try it. But if I don't like her—'

'Thank you,' Mum smiles. 'Thank you, love.'

She links her arm in mine, and with a forgiving shove, Beth does the same with Chad.

'Come on, provisional driver.'

O ▫ THE FOOL

A week can be a long time when you're grounded, so it's the greatest thing when I get the text. I stare at my phone screen for what seems like hours.

Hey, Sam,

Few of us going to ZubZub tonight. Maybe see you there?

x

That X. A bullet through my heart. And while I reel, right on cue, I get another text from Chad.

Zub tonight, mate!

I'm grounded, but so NEED this!

Meet you at your back gate, usual spot 10 pm.

I watch from my bedroom window and see it, a flash from Chad's phone. We've done this so many times over the years, creeping out at night for a laugh. We've been careful, though, always back in bed before dawn. Because we know if we're caught, our little adventures would be over for good.

Chad's phone flashes again. I pull my shoes on.

The stone sits on the windowsill, a moon against the cold night. I get that feeling that it's watching, waiting for me.

'All right, strange stone, you can come too.'

I slip it into my jacket, and swing the window open. In a few seconds, I'm onto the drainpipe and shinning down, quiet as a mouse, into our little garden.

I can hear the television. Mum's watching the news. Beth's bedroom light is on. All the neighbours' windows with their blinds down, little slivers of white, as if the houses are slumbering. A low hoot sounds above me, and I see a shape swoop across the starry sky. An owl on the hunt. For mousey me?

'Oi, what you looking at?' Chad's urgent whisper. 'Come on!'

I sprint through the dark, and we're off, laughing like hyenas, swallowed by the night.

The bus into town is empty. We're on the top floor, at the back.

'Sorry about the police station, mate. Never thought we'd get caught.'

But I sense him giggling and then I'm giggling too, trying to hold it back, like when you're in fits in class, and it just makes it worse and funnier.

'Your face,' Chad points at me, holding his sides.

'*Your* face, you mean!'

The bus brakes and we clutch to the rails, sailors riding a storm.

'Come on, our stop.'

Downstairs the doors clatter open. I'm feeling so happy to be out with Chad, to know that I'm going to see Oona. This'll be an epic night.

'Watch it!'

A group of lads barrels into us, all bodies and laughs.

'Well, if it isn't Sammy boy Mitchell.'

There's only one person who calls me that. He steps forward, hoody up against the bright bus hoarding. Dan McGuire. This isn't good. Ever since primary we've rubbed each other up the wrong way. I feel Chad pull on my arm.

'Bit past your bedtime, isn't it?' Dan rubs his chin, a black scruff of beard. I feel the eyes of his tittering mates on me. Dan flipping McGuire. All those years back, when I stopped him picking on a new boy called Chad Harding, the boy who murmurs to me now.

'Come on, Sam...'

But Dan puts his body in the way. He's bigger than me now. Bet I'm still faster, though. Like I always was at school sports, leaving him shouting in my wake.

'Where you two going? Gay bar, is it?'

More tittering. I reach into my pocket for the stone.

'Leave it, Dan,' I say, and my hand tenses, ready to draw.

'*Leave it, Dan*,' he mimics, in a baby voice. 'Or what, Sammy boy? You'll give me a lesson?'

Blue lights sweep across his mocking face, and I see his eyes drop. There's a police car idling beside us.

'See you around, Sammy boy.'

Dan's shoulder shoves mine, and they're off, a huddle of hoodies slipping away like a pack of black dogs.

'He doesn't change, does he?' laughs Chad, but with more of a tremble than a chuckle.

I look at him, seeing that scared boy held by the throat, and we move on, away from the shining eyes of Dan and his stupid gang.

I don't care about them. There's a club to find and fun to be had.

'Sam! Chad! Over here!'

The boys – Darren, Timbo, Ben and Sharkey – are in the queue. Their breath steams under the cheesy purple neon that pulses 'ZubZub' on the wall.

'Man, it's so cold!' Big Ben stamps his big feet, looking over heads.

Sharkey points from under his fringe. 'Stag do, look.'

At the door there's a group of blokes kitted out like Vikings, with huge horned helmets and plastic swords, one wears an L-plate.

'Benjy, he's bigger than you!' Darren points at another bloke, a robe over his broad shoulders, a long wig under his wide-brimmed hat. 'Hurry up, mate! Valhalla will be closed soon!'

And we burst out laughing, as the queue flows forward under the lights, and my belly buzzes, because it feels so good, the hum of the club drawing us into that warm blackness, descending stairs we can't see. I think of Dad telling me the story of Hades, the brooding god of the underworld. And I think about Oona. My Persephone in the dark.

The life bringer, Sam. Her light shining from the shadows.

She's light all right, Dad. The most beautiful light I've ever seen.

We're sucked into a whirl of dry ice and noise, in the club proper now and there are people everywhere, whooping and twisting to the beat.

'Yesssss!' Chad jumps in among the boys, hands in the air and blue-white smiles. 'Sam! Come on, man!' He pulls me through, and deeper we go into the bouncing crowd, as the DJ bellows and everyone shrieks for more.

And there they are.

Chloe and Gina laughing back-to-back, Tash waving to us. There, there she is, and it seems like the flashing lights are only on her as she turns and smiles, lightning striking me, making me cry out.

'Oona!'

I push forward. Towards that smile. Those dark eyes casting their spell.

'Sam!'

She shouts my name, not Chad's, or Ben's, or Sharkey's. Mine.

She reaches her hand through the crowd, for me and only me. And as I stretch for her perfect white fingers, I think of Dad. If he had lived to see this girl of my dreams.

A body steps across me, blocks out the light.

'All right?' he shouts at Oona. 'What's your name?'

It's Dan. I turn to see the leer of his dog boys.

'Oi!' I move to go past him, get back to Oona.

'Let's dance!' Dan snatches her reaching hand. No.

I shoulder him. Hard. He totters away. Oona's eyes are wide.

'Don't worry – just a drunk—'

Suddenly I'm flying sideways.

Vikings all around. Lights and legs and looks.

Hands like iron lift me. It's the big guy from outside, a plastic patch over one eye. Odins everywhere.

'Rise, my warrior!' His grin is bright violet.

Instinctively, I reach for the stone in my pocket.

A girl dances by, black feathers in her hair.

Flash.

Flash.

Flash.

Oona.

I dive back through the crowd, the music shaking my bones. And I see Dan with his arm around Oona. I see her pushing him away.

My fingers grip, the stone bites.

'Dan!'

He swivels, his muscled arm swings. But he's slow.

Flash.

Flash.

I dance aside, the beat in my blood.

Flash.

And I throw my fist curled about a burning stone, but a hand catches, pulls it down.

'Right! Out! Now!'

I'm being hauled by someone with arms like a vice.

'He started it!'

'Move!'

The bouncers lift me through the dancers, all lost to the music.

'Get off me!'

I turn, to see my friends' faces, white and worried.

'You're barred.' I'm forced up the stairs onto the street.

'But my mates are in there!'

'Should've thought of that. Hop it!'

'Sam!'

Oona and Chad at the door. Sharkey and Darren close behind. Chloe and Gina straining to see.

'What are you all staring at?'

'How you do that, mate?' Sharkey says. 'You were so fast...'

I move the stone behind my back.

'Oona, you okay?' My voice shakes. It's not the cold.

She just nods and looks at me like everyone else. As if I'm a mad dog about to bite.

'Sam, mate – let me take you home.'

'No, forget it!'

I kick at the bins.

'That's enough, lad.' A bouncer steps forward. 'Leave or I'm calling the police.'

'All right, I'm going – leave me alone!' They stop and watch me, like my friends watch me, like Oona watches me. 'All of you, leave me alone!'

I cut and run.

The park is dark and rain hisses through the trees. A lonely street light flickers above a bench. I can make out someone, under an umbrella, a dog at their side.

I don't know what led me here. I just had to get somewhere.

'What are you all staring at?'

'You were so fast...'

That look on Oona's face. I pull out my phone, start to message her.

Shouts behind me. Getting nearer.

Oona, I'm...

'Sammyyy boyyyy!'

I turn to see four hooded figures. They move apart, and the middle one steps out.

'You always were a fast little thing.'

My fingers find the stone in my pocket. It's like reaching for a gun.

'Leave me alone.' The rain flattens my voice.

'Dan, mate.' Another lad leans in. 'We doing this, or what?'

Dan runs rubs his hand across his chin. 'Heard all about your dad, Sammy boy.'

The rain smacks off their stupid hoods.

'Yeah.' He shows his big teeth like a horse. 'I know all about your poor daddy...'

'Shut up.' My whisper trembles, anger quickening.

The dog lads are a creeping circle. I back away, turning between them.

'In the desert, wasn't it? Wasn't he driving?'

'I said, shut up!'

My hand draws from my pocket, becomes a fist.

'What's the matter, mate? Can't take it?'

'That they blew up...'

I feel the snarl boil through my belly—

'... your stupid...'

Into my bones, bursting from me.

'... dad!'

'SHUT UP!'

I lunge, roaring with rage.

His fist crashes into my chest, knocks me flying. Air vomits from my lungs. I roll in the mud and they're on me. Men-boys who kick my back, punch my head, whose shouts rain down upon me.

'Hit me, would you, Sammy boy? This hiding's been a long time coming!'

A kick to my ear makes it burn. I roll as another boy takes aim. Enough of this. I grasp the stone and I fling, finding soft belly.

'Uuuh!'

He groans, landing heavy in the mud.

I'm on my feet, springing fast.

Another takes a swing. I leap, my muscles whip, as I kick, bring a whine of pain.

'Hey, you!'

I hurl my fist, an arrow through the rain. Dan reaching for me. But I reach him first. He howls, holding his face.

My hand sings, blood spills.

'You! I'll kill you!' He spits blood. 'What's in your hand?'

'Stop, I said, all of you!'

There is a policewoman, an old man, a dog.

'Dan, come on!'

Those pups pull at their master who points at me. At the stone I hold.

'Look at that!'

'I know you – Dan McGuire...' The policewoman steps forward.

His pack pull him from the ground.

'Are you all right, son?' The old man is close.

'I'll give you a stone! You wait!'

'Dan, run!'

'I'll give you a flamin' stone!' He bolts. 'Just you wait!'

'I saw them come at you, lad.'

I blink at the old man, then look out across the park.

'Good thing this constable was driving by.'

'Are you all right?' asks the policewoman. 'Your hand...'

I look through a haze at my knuckles. Pain fizzes and burns. I shove my hand away, bury the stone.

'We should get you looked at. What's your name?'

'I'm okay...' I feel drained. Not police again. Got to go. How did I get here?

'Lad, let us help you—'

'No, no. I'm okay...'

I slip in the scuffed mud, as the rain splatters and smacks.

They're all watching me, the old man and the policewoman. Even the dog. So I do what I have to do.

I leg it.

And I don't look back as I run on through that hissing, sodden park.

E arly morning. Rain clatters through a cold dawn. It's horrible.

Mostly it's horrible because of what happened in the night.

My head and my hand ache, but was any of last night real? How could it be?

'What the flip are you?' I say to the stone lying on my bedside table.

It says nothing, of course. Still as stone. My phone buzzes and I nearly fall out of bed reaching for it. It's Chad.

Hope you're okay, bud...

We went soon after you.

Not much fun for some reason! ;->

Give us a shout when you're up.

I start to text, then stop. Because I'm thinking of their faces under that purple light of the club. All my friends staring at me. With the same look in their eyes.

Fright. Fear. Worry.

Especially Oona, looking at me with eyes that hurt my heart.

I message her.

I'm sorry about last night. It

It what? It's that I keep seeing things, but then it might be all in my head, and there's this magic stone in my pocket...

There is such a thing as too much information.

... would be good to see you later?

And I pause again, wondering if I should. But she started it, so I go for it.

X

I press send and wait – will – for that typing heartbeat. But nothing. Flatline.

I put my phone next to the stone, and think about her dancing.

Think about her reaching for me, her smile only for me.

I think about Oona, as I fall back to sleep.

Mum and Beth are talking in the kitchen. They stop as I enter. Ambushed again.

'Good night, big brother?'

She winks, which is a relief, as we haven't spoken much in the last few days.

'Slept okay, if that's what you mean.' I pour out some

cereal. Mum passes me the milk.

Beth plucks some cornflakes from my bowl.

'Oh, right,' she crunches, her eyes flicking over to Mum, 'that's *so* what I mean.'

She knows. No hiding anything ever from Beth.

'We're not stupid, Sam,' says Mum. She looks as if she hasn't slept for days. 'We know you've been out. We've known for ages.'

The flakes float in my mouth. I see them both look at my hand, the red glare of the bruise. I can still feel Dan's chin as I struck it.

'Oh, what have you done, love?' Mum reaches for me, and I see that same Mum who would scoop me up from a bump and kiss it better.

'Nothing, Mum!' My hand stings, so I grasp for a lie. 'Just want to finish this – I'm late for Chad.'

'But you've got your appointment with Dr Fellowes today, remember?'

For a moment I don't know who she's talking about, I swallow milk and flakes.

'Oh… yeah, yeah …'

'Will you talk to her about what happened with your dad that ni—?'

'Oh God, Mum. Not this!' I duck away. I can see it hurts her, but it hurts even more to talk about, so I yank the back door, dive out.

Beth's right behind me.

'I know you're not meeting Chad.'

'How do you know?'

She pauses as though she's going to say something, then grabs me instead.

'At the hospital – what happened?'

'Nothing!'

'This is me, remember!' She pulls. She's strong. 'What's with that rock you're carrying around?'

'What… rock?' I blink back my lie.

'Sam, what's going on?'

I push her hands away, as she gives me a Beth stare, lasering for the truth. I always tell her everything. But not this, I can't. I head down the path.

'Sam!' Mum's next to Beth. 'I know you think you have to deal with this on your own. But you don't. We're here…' Drizzle spots her dress, as she smiles, shakily. 'We're always here for you.'

'Mum, Beth, I…'

So many things rush through me that I want to tell them. How bad it felt to bury Dad. How good I feel when I see Oona. How I'm seeing things, feeling things that I can't explain. That frighten me and thrill me too.

'I can't talk now.'

'Then talk to her, Sam,' Mum says. 'For us.'

Beth draws her back, still searchlighting me under that frown she's had all her life. She won't stop till she's got it out of me, and that frightens me the most.

So like the scaredy-cat I am, I turn away and slope off through the rain.

✳

'Hi, Sam, I'm Rachel…'

The therapist smiles, offering her hand. She's in a room with two big armchairs facing each other, a coffee table between them, with glasses of water, a box of tissues.

'Please. Have a seat…'

I sit and she sits, pushing back her blonde hair. A notepad and pen waits on the arm of her chair. She's younger than I expected. But then I didn't know what to expect. Like I didn't expect to be here.

'So, you know your mother contacted me. While you were in hospital?'

I nod.

'And how's your head, now?'

'Physically or mentally?'

She smiles, letting her pen hover.

'You tell me, Sam.'

I look at the box of tissues, waiting to be plucked. Not by me.

'My head's fine.'

Rachel's pen marks her pad. I even get notes for being okay. I just need to get through this. One session and it's done. I'll tell Mum we didn't get on, that she wasn't right.

'Sam, why do you think your mother asked for us to meet?'

I shrug and look around the room. There are shelves with books, a window onto a huge horse chestnut tree, its leaves turning deep amber. On the wall, a picture of a little circus dog balancing on a white ball. I remember the white of Odin's eye.

The stone.

It's everywhere. I feel it inside my jacket. Like I've got a prize conker from that old tree. A sixer and no mistake.

'Sam, do you remember what happened?' Rachel's steady gaze returns me to the room. 'Before hospital. What happened in the library?'

The library. Odin in the book. That memory of Dad returning so strongly.

... the god of the wild hunt, leading fallen warriors...

'I... don't remember much.'

Apart from seeing my father. As clear as Rachel is to me now.

'I just fainted.'

Rachel nods, her pen dancing.

'The consultant at the hospital told me you sustained light concussion. Nothing that a few days' rest won't sort, but I hear from your family that you had another fall... after the funeral.'

We've come to it. The F-word.

'That was nothing. I was running with Alfie – that's our dog...' I'm talking quickly, as Rachel keeps nodding. 'I was running and I tripped over him and fell. I didn't black out or anything. I just fell.'

I stop lying, my eyes darting away to the picture of the little dog. I think about Alfie barking over and over.

As the owl fell for me. The wind rushing against my body.

Rachel leans forward. 'Do you remember why you were running, Sam?'

I look back at her sharply.

'You mean, was I running from my dad's death?'

'Would that be so bad?'

My chest feels constricted. I'm breathing fast. It's hot.

'Sam, do you want a drink?'

She pours a glass of water, filling it with light from the window. The tree moves in the water. Like that gorse bush. Sun on the stone when I reached for it. When I saw Dad.

'No. I don't.' I stand up clumsily, knocking the table.

Light moves in the gorse. The stone waits for me.

'I've… I've got to go.'

I move towards the door and Rachel watches me like a wolf, about to pounce.

'You can't stop me.'

She puts down her pad.

'No, Sam, I can't, but—' A huge yawn catches her. 'Oh my goodness…' She pulls a few tissues.

I watch her dab her eyes and tuck a tissue into her sleeve, the way Mum does.

'I'm sorry, that was unprofessional.' She looks up, restored. 'No rest for the wicked.'

'What does that mean?'

We're both surprised as my words jump from me.

Rachel hesitates. 'I shouldn't say... Well, what's the harm. My son. He's teething terribly.'

I picture her rocking a bawling baby. Suddenly she's not a doctor trying to grill me.

'Doesn't make you a bad mum, though.'

I think of mine, stroking my cheek. Alone and sad. And I've not been helping lately.

'That's a relief,' says Rachel. 'You know, I always thought it was unfair on the stepmothers in fairy tales. Always evil and plotting.'

She stands and goes to the window. The horse chestnut waves its brown arms.

'I loved *Rumplestiltskin* when I was a little girl. Something so deliciously dark about it, that little old man.' She watches the tree, listening to the creak of a spinning wheel in a locked tower room.

'And what about you, Sam?'

'What about me?'

'Did you have a favourite fairy tale?'

I'm back in bed with Dad reading to me and Beth, as the wind whips outside, and it's so warm and safe with him, that nothing will get us, no harm will come, not while he's there with us. Not while he's our dad.

'*Hansel and Gretel.*' I lick my lips. Should have had that water.

'Can you remember the thing... the one thing you loved so much about it?'

I watch her. She doesn't seem to be trapping me. Fairy tales are easy to talk about.

'I liked...'

I think about Hansel's cleverness, a trail of breadcrumbs and white pebbles through the dark woods. I think about a magic house made of sweets, too good to be true. I think about a sly witch, hungry for children. How they tricked her with a chicken bone for a finger, and a hot oven slammed shut, and how those children ran and ran for their lives. I tremble, feeling a witch at my back, and then I know, what it was I loved so much and so did Beth, why we always wanted Dad to tell us, please tell us.

'It's about a brother and sister...'

Rachels smiles and nods.

'They're on their own. It's dangerous. But together, they get away. Back to safety and their father.'

I watch as Rachel's eyes light and she moves back to her pad.

'Are you going to write that down?'

Her pen's in her hand. 'Do you mind if I do?'

It's warm in here. Like a witch's oven.

'Why, though?'

'Because I liked it.' She looks at me straight and true. 'And because I want to help you.'

So a trick all along.

'Well, write this down. They find their father and live happily ever after. But mine is dead. The end.'

Need to get out, can't breathe. I pull at the door handle behind me.

'Sam, wait a minute—'

It doesn't move. 'Why is this locked?'

'The handle's stiff, Sam—'

I tug, the door springs open. I step out.

'Hello there!'

I nearly jump out of my skin.

There's an old man sitting, waiting. My heart bangs as he smiles at me.

'My turn, is it?'

He starts to stand, creaking up from his chair. Then I realise, I've seen him before. It's the old man from the park, the fight with Dan and his dogs.

'We're a bit early, Bill, but come through.' Rachel is next to me. 'Sam – Bill.'

'We've met, haven't we, Sam?' He winks and grins, showing bright white dentures beneath brown, freckled skin. 'How's that hand, lad?'

His accent is rich and Northern. Lancashire, like Wallace and Gromit.

'It's okay, thanks…' I cover my bruised hand and step aside. As he passes, I get a waft of hair oil from the thin strands of Bill's combed hair. There's a neat 'tache across his top lip, from another time, from old black and white films. A whine from the corridor and a squat, grey-flecked dog watches us, eyes rheumy with age.

'I've had to bring Badger today, Rachel – he's being a

right pain.' Then to me, 'You left a bit sharpish when we met, lad. I've been worried about you.'

I sense Rachel looking at me, questions rising. 'I'm... I'm fine...'

The dog Badger gives another long whine.

Bill tuts. 'I can't have you doing that for the next hour.' He puts his wrinkled hand on mine. 'Do you have a dog, Sam?'

'Yes... Yes, I do.'

'Then how about one good turn deserving another? Could you walk Badger down the park?'

The old dog's ears prick at that magic word.

'You want me to walk your dog?'

'Well, I can't leave him outside.' Bill hands me a sodden lead and poo bags. 'You best get a move on or you'll miss kick-off.'

'What... kick-off?' I blink at this strange old man.

'The local match on the rec, you daft apeth! Meet you there for second half.'

Badger shuffles and pants. I'm standing there like a lemon. How many ambushes can I get in one day? And what's an 'apeth'?

'What a lovely idea, Sam.' Rachel smiles. 'I'll be right with you, Bill.'

'Right you are. Right you are...' He nods and waves as Rachel takes a step into the corridor.

'Sam, I want to say something before you leave...'

I watch the old man sink into that big armchair. He

smiles at me, then he winks again. He must be in his eighties.

'I wanted to say, I was simply getting to know you. In that room, there's no agenda, no point scoring. It's about talking about anything you want and…' Her voice lowers to a whisper. 'I'm sorry about the warmth – Bill feels the cold a bit.' She pulls the door, but I can still see Bill's huge white grin. What's he doing here?

'If you come back, I promise I'll turn it down, and I promise we can talk about anything you want, Sam.'

Now that is a promise. Because we have so much territory to cover. Visits from my dead father. A stone that makes me strong, makes me see through the eyes of animals. Visions of unknown girls. Not forgetting Odin, the watcher of the dead. Who Beth called my dad's 'favourite god', who came to visit us on the hill, years before my father became one of his fallen warriors. Why, yes, we could fill Mrs Pratt's library with all this material, me and Rachel. But looking at that smiling old man getting comfy, something occurs to me. I can come to this room and just be still. Nothing chasing me. I can hide away, just be.

And like he can read my thoughts, Bill gives me the thumbs-up.

'Okay, Rachel.' I turn to go. 'I hope you get some sleep.'

'Thank you, Sam.' She smiles. 'Sorry to keep you, Bill…'

Her door closes, and I leave my first therapy session with Dr Rachel Fellowes, PhD, psychotherapy practitioner and young mother, as I'm pulled to my fate by a dog called Badger.

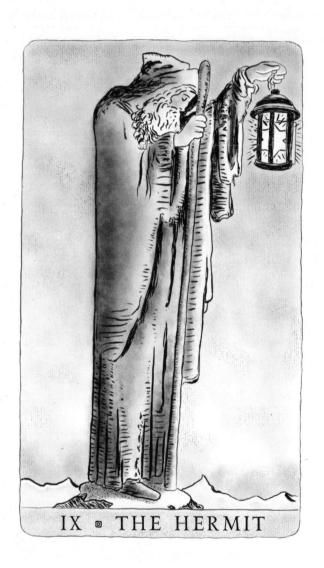

IX ◉ THE HERMIT

'PEEEEP!'

The ref blows and the reds kick-off against the blues, the eternal battle.

Badger whines at my feet. I pull my jacket in. How did I get into this, standing watching a football match in the October cold, looking after some bloke's old dog? But I know full well. Bill had me blackmailed well and good. I owed him for his silence.

'Come on, son! Move yourself!'

A bald guy bellows across the pitch. A competitive father. Then, right on cue, Dad steps onto the touchline, into my thoughts. He'd bring me to this pitch when I was in the primary school footie team. I remember how he would stamp his feet on the frozen winter ground, his Irish brogue ringing out cheers and curses.

One time it was so cold he brought a little flask of whisky. He gave me a nip at half time. I can still taste that sting of fiery liquid as it went down my throat and burned my belly.

I check my phone. Nothing from Oona. Is she annoyed with me? My thumb hovers, just as Badger pulls and barks, his tail going like the clappers, and a voice rings out.

'I'm coming as fast as I can, you old sausage!'

Coming along the side of the pitch, Bill walks with a slight limp, a bag at his side and he waves.

'Ey up, Sam!'

'Um... Hi...'

Badger fusses, whining and licking his gnarled hands. You'd think his master had been gone for years.

'Hold your horses, daft dog, I'm getting it, if you'll give me a tick...'

He takes a thermos out of his beaten-up bag. Both bag and thermos have a tartan pattern.

'Here you go, then...'

I watch as Bill fills the thermos mug with steaming tea and places it on the ground. Badger bolts, lapping furiously.

'He likes... tea?'

Bill chuckles. 'Loves it, don't you, you old thing? Not as much as half a bitter, though!'

Badger lifts his dribbling chops, then dives back in, tea sloshing about his ears, as his master strokes his mottled fur. I get this sudden rush, that Badger is all Bill has, that it won't be for ever, and it's stupid but I feel sad for them.

It's probably the dog, reminds me of Alfie. Dogs don't live long, and we give them all our love.

'Here, there's a good drop left...'

Bill sloshes tea into another mug and hands it to me. Boys shriek past on BMXs.

'Thanks...'

The tea is sweet and hot.

'So?'

I look up at him.

'What?'

'What, he says! What's with all that nonsense the other night what?' He nods at my bruises. 'Who were those boys?'

A cheer goes up. The reds hurry to hug the goal-scorer who does that shirt over the head thing, arms aloft, soaring in celebration.

'Just school mates...'

'Mates, my bony behind! I know a fight when I see one.' Now Badger's eyeing me too. Two old fellas giving me the third degree. 'What was it all about, lad?'

Nothing, I'm about to say, but I can see Bill's having none of it.

'Drugs? This county lines business, I'm reading about?'

'No!' I spit tea.

'Owe money, then?'

'No, it's not – look, I really need to—'

'Ah!' Bill grips my arm. It's like being grappled by a

skeleton. 'Then there's got to be a lass involved I'd wager. Am I right?'

And Bill's sent me back to the club, as I pushed to get to Oona. When Dan stepped between us. I feel the twitch of anger in my belly as he leered at her, *'All right? What's your name?'*

'Kind of...'

Then I'm thinking about the park last night. What he said about Dad. I can barely remember the fight. Just grunts and howls.

A blue yells and rolls in agony, a red shouts at the ref.

'What's her name?'

Bill strokes Badger's head and his stubby tail thumps the bench.

'Oona.'

'Oh, Oona, is it? Well, I hope Oona's worth the trouble.'

I remember Dan shouting as he ran into the rain, 'I'll give you a flamin' stone!'

This wasn't the end of it. Not if I knew anything about Dan McGuire.

Bill's eyes meet mine. 'It's none of my business, Sam, but are you in trouble? Do you need help, lad?'

He presses my arm. He's so weird, this little man who suddenly wants to help me.

'No.' I extract myself from his grip. 'I'm... I'm fine. Honest.'

Badger snorts as a gust of wind pushes leaves across the

pitch, tumbling them over the players' boots. And again I get an impression of this old man and his dog. That in their loneliness, all they've got left is each other. For all Bill's grins and winks, there's a sadness there, blowing through him.

'Why... why are you going to see Rachel?'

He pauses, mug half-raised.

'Why are you?'

Psychotherapy poker. Right then, I'll call his bluff.

'My dad died.'

Bill nods, pulling on Badger's fur.

'My wife died.'

The old dog leans on my leg. He's muscly and heavy like a retired boxer.

'And...' Bill licks lips cracked with wrinkles, 'I see her all the time.'

I start and look at him, as he sips at his tea, watching the footballers shout and run.

'You're seeing her? How?'

He watches me back, as if he's weighing me up.

'I'm not rightly sure. I just get this... this sense of her...'

And I'm thinking of Dad now. Dad saluting me in the road as the school bus passed. Dad in the dark of the library. Dad haunting me.

'It happens mostly when I come down the stairs.' Bill swills his tea. 'May will often be sitting on the sofa. It's funny, I never actually see her, because when I look up there's no one there, but it's a feeling I have, you know, an instinct that there's someone sitting on the sofa. And I just know it's her in that moment. Something in the way she sits, as if she's waiting for me to come down, waiting to ask if I want a brew and get up for the kettle. I get this complete whiff of her, you know? But no sooner do I look at that sofa, than my heart gives this little jump – always catches me off guard – always when I look up, she's not there. It's as though if I don't look at her, she's there, but if I do then she's not. Bloody typical woman!'

A cheer comes from across the park and the blues jump for joy.

'One all.' Bill nods. 'Up the blues.'

In my mind, I see Bill on his stairs, his wrinkled hand on the banister as he looks at the empty sofa. I want to say something comforting to him, but I can't think of anything that hasn't been said before. Then it just comes out in a surge I can't stop.

'I see... I see my dad.'

'Oh?'

His eyes may be old and watery, but they're bright and clear. For an instant, I wonder what he was like when he was my age.

'And does he drive you potty like my May? Being there and not there?'

'No. No, it's not like that... I really see him. I see him everywhere.'

I pause, because I should feel stupid, but I don't. I feel I can tell this funny little old man anything and everything.

'And how does that make you feel, Sam?'

His fingers have crept back to my arm. But I leave them this time. I've not told Bill the real reason. That I've been seeing Dad ever since I found the stone.

'Well, he's dead...'

'So it frightens you?'

'No, 'course not.'

He watches me steady.

'I'm happy to see him, but...'

I feel my arm shake under his pressing fingers.

'But then I think, he's not really there. He's gone. And so I... So... I...'

'You miss him more.'

Badger sits up with a growl. A squirrel bounds down from a tree.

'Yes.' I nod, pushing the hurt back.

Bill strokes Badger, who's looking more alert than I've seen all day. 'I come to this pitch a lot, Sam. Because this is where May and I would watch the world go by. When I'm here, it's like I'm next to her, our shoulders touching...'

Badger stands with a crick of his old legs. The squirrel watches him, twitching.

'Do you have a place like that? Somewhere special?'

I think about when we strode out across the ridgeway, as if we were the only people left on the planet. As if we could keep walking and walking. All those times, from when I was little, and he was Dadhorse, carrying me on his back. Countless times as I grew up. Our times, just Dad and me together. A red kite hovering above. A hare streaking away. I never wanted it to stop, never wanted to come home. And, of course, there was our place, our favourite place.

'The White Horse at the top of the ridgeway, where the old iron age fort was…'

Bill's hand closes on mine.

'Well, that's where you'll always find him, lad. Like here on this bench with my May. That place is where your worlds touch.'

I'm fighting so hard now to keep tears away, and Bill knows. He can see what I'm battling with, because he's the same. He's an old man weeping in front of an empty sofa, watched by his old dog.

'Would you show me, Sam? Could we walk up there, me and you?'

I look at him, and his dog, at the hollering players and the dancing squirrel. I look at this teeming life around me and I want to shout out suddenly for it all. I want to shout about how alive we are, that the dead are dead and they stay like that.

But instead, I take Bill's cold old hand in mine and squeeze it as I smile.

'It would be a pleasure —'

My phone buzzes. It's Oona! At last!

Meet me at Loxdale stables, tomorrow 2pm?

'Sorry, hang on…' I start to write back, feeling Bill's

eyes on me.

Yes! See you there!

My mind churning. Stables? I stare at that little typing heartbeat, feeling the buzz of knowing she's there, connected to me.

Great. I'll sort you a horse. X

'Oh my God… I can't ride a horse!'

I only realise I've said that out loud when I hear Bill's hacking laugh.

'She's got you good, son!'

He claps me on the back and laughs again as Badger woofs and lollops towards a squirrel that he'll never catch.

'I would say things are looking up, wouldn't you, Sam?'

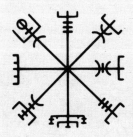

Ten days since we buried you.

Of all the photos in our house, there's the one I keep coming back to.

It's of you and Mum on your wedding day.

You're pointing to the confetti on your big nose.

Mum's clinging to you, laughing her socks off.

And clasped tight and safe.

Your fingers are banded in gold.

Full of promise and promises.

I love this photo, because this was your time.

Where you'll hold each other for ever.

VI ⊙ THE LOVERS

The horse looks down its long nose at me.

'Sam, this is Barney.'

Oona smiles from beneath her helmet and strokes the white patch on that bobbing nose.

'And, Barney, this is Sam.'

I watch her lead the horse out of its stable, its hooves loud and massive on the cobbles.

'I thought you were joking...'

I watch those terrifying legs stamp, as it snorts.

'*Shhh...*' Oona soothes and calms this giant animal, all grace and power, sunlight bouncing off its flanks. 'Barney's no joke, are you, my love?'

She whispers and strokes and Barney steadies. I get a flash of envy watching them.

'So how long've you been doing this?'

'Oh, from back in Ireland, when I was little.' Oona adjusts the horse's bridle, and I see her mind wander. 'My father used to say...' She laughs and her smile is like the dawn breaking over faraway hills. 'He used to say I must learn so I could ride with the witches at full moon.' I get a sudden flash of Oona on horseback, galloping with those girls I saw on the hill.

'Come on. Enough time-wasting.'

'Come on, what?'

But Oona just rolls her eyes, and plonks a helmet in my hands. Then she turns to the stable next to Barney's and pulling the half door, releases a flurry of white mane and muscle into the yard.

'And this is Snowdrop.'

'Snowbeast more like,' I croak. It's as if the White Horse has sprung from the land, a deity towering over me.

In one swift movement, Oona flows up into the saddle. Snowdrop looks at me as though I'm a complete idiot.

'Grab up, there...' She points to the raised front of Barney's saddle, then to the stirrup that seems about a mile off the ground. 'Your left foot there... pull up and swing over.'

'That simple, eh?' I say clipping the itchy, heavy helmet under my chin.

Oona reaches to hold Barney, one perfect paint-stroke eyebrow curling into a question.

'Okay... Okay...'

I jump for the saddle front, and, just about sticking my foot in that high stirrup, I huff and puff my way upwards. It seems to take for ever, finally yanking my leg over Barney's wide back. I breathe out, glad to be at the summit.

'Use the reins to guide and your heels to squeeze gently, but Barney knows where he's going.'

Oona turns the mighty Snowdrop towards the open gates, and Barney snorts and nods, his powerful shoulders moving under me as we start to move.

'Whoa!'

I catch my balance, clutching his thick mane.

'Stop worrying. You'll enjoy it!' Oona laughs and clicks her tongue. Snowdrop carries her like a queen out of the stable yard. Green fields and black trees beckon, and in the near distance the call of the hills.

'Okay, Barney. Go easy, boy.'

I try to click my tongue like Oona, but it sounds rubbish. Barney snorts, because he doesn't need orders from me, and he saunters into a trot, his back bumping my bum into the air, as together we ride out, following Snowdrop into the autumn blue.

We climb a rise, keeping to a worn old bridle path, as the October wind blows over the hill to find us. I have walked here with Dad so many times, taking paths that have been trodden for centuries and more. But not since his funeral. When everything changed.

'What are you thinking, Sam?'

Snowdrop huffs beside Barney. Over Oona's shoulder I spy the roofs of our village, little toy houses spilled below us.

'That it's good to get away from everything,' I lie. I don't want to talk to her about Dad. I want some time for us.

She nods.

'Sam, that fight at the nightclub…'

'It wasn't really a fight,' I say too quickly, guiltily thinking of what happened later with Dan and his pack.

'You really shoved that guy.'

'I was only trying to get to you.'

She leans back, her hand on my arm.

'Sam, it's not on, I tell you.'

'But—'

'Do you think girls like that?'

'No, I was—'

'So, you're not going to do it again, are you?'

Dan swaggers into my mind.

'No, 'course not.'

And he sneers at my second lie. For Dan McGuire it's never over, since I pushed him off Chad all those years ago.

Barney's hoof slips and I heave forwards.

'Whoa!'

Oona steadies me.

'He's just kicking over rocks. You won't fall.'

I touch her hand, cold from the wind.

'You're freezing. Here.'

She blushes as I hold her palm in mine, as our horses

walk on. This is the moment. I have to go for it. I have to, or I never will.

'Did you hear there's a Halloween rave soon, up at the White Horse?'

I motion ahead to the next couple of rises, feeling her soft skin under my fingers.

'I heard – isn't it all us girls talk about?' she laughs, and blushes again. 'Where I'm from, I don't call it Halloween.' She looks down at her hand in mine. 'Samhain is how I know it – Summer's End'. She peers up to the sky where two rooks croak on the wind. 'When all that's dead returns to the earth.'

I shiver. 'Samhain is what my dad called it too.' I stop, butting into Dad again. 'It's fancy dress, the party.' I grin. 'Should be good.'

Snowdrop shifts his bulk away, and our arms stretch, but I don't let go.

'Long ago…' she stares ahead to where the White Horse waits, 'it was said the souls of the dead would come home, to sit at the table during Samhain.' The rooks circle, we're all listening to Oona. 'And people would celebrate this, by dressing up, going door to door in exchange for food.'

'Trick or treat,' I say and tug at her fingers.

'More like apples and nuts.'

She looks back at me, almost as if she's travelled up to the hill and back, a priestess breaking her trance.

Snowdrop trots forward, our hands pull apart. I want to shout.

'Come on!' she calls. 'Bring Barney on, give him a little dig!' The great horse beneath her lengthens its stride. 'Let's get to the top and see the view!'

'Oona, wait!'

But she's away, trotting up the path.

'Wait!' But Barney's already moving faster. I have to catch her. To ask her. 'Come on, boy!' Rashly, I kick a bit too hard, and Barney gives a whinny, leaping forward.

The breath jumps from my lungs and I drop the reins to clutch his mane.

'Whoa!'

But he doesn't whoa. He's moving faster. And we're passing Oona.

'Sam! Pull hard on the reins! Sit back in the saddle!'

Barney thunders on, and I'm desperately holding his neck.

'Sam!'

The sun is sharp in my eyes. All I can hear is wind, the great breaths of the horse.

Oona calls, but I can only hold on for dear life as we speed towards a gate.

I think about Dad. How he would know what to do.

'Dad!'

So I reach for the stone because – because he might come.

'Dad!'

I grip it as hard as I grip that mane as I grip the memory of him.

'Dad, please!'

The ground is rushing past,

I look down.

At two wolves who stand and stare with hungry eyes.

Barney comes to a sudden stop and I'm hurled out of the saddle.

I hit the ground, and I'm rolling and rolling, pain hammering.

'Sam!'

Oona's close, I hear hooves and I think that's it, I'm done. But at least I can go with Dad. If the wolves don't eat me first.

'Sam? Are you okay?'

'The wolves...'

'What?' Quickly she ties up the horses.

'Have the wolves gone?'

'Sam, there's nothing.' Oona looks down at me, her hair slipping from her helmet, and she puts a hand to my face, her warmth soothing the pain. 'Barney bolted. And you fell. Are you hurt?'

I reach up to her, touch her cheek. She's amazing.

'Will you... come to the party with me?'

She stares down at me, then she laughs. 'Of all the ways to get my attention!'

'Will you, Oona?'

'Yes! All right, all right, you maniac!' She shoves me and the stone drops from my hand. She stops laughing, staring at it.

'Sam, where did you get that?'

The stone rolls on the grass and the rooks cry out.

'I… I found it.' I think about that strange, awful day. Burying Dad. Seeing him on the hill. 'Near to here.'

Oona reaches for the stone.

'Wait…'

But she's too fast, and the stone is in her hand.

'A scrying stone…' Her dark eyes light. 'I never thought I would see one…'

'You know what this is?'

'The witches used them in their magick.' She turns the stone, smoothing it. 'To tell the future, to read the past…' she looks back at me, 'to open other worlds.'

A scrying stone. Witches.

'Oona… I think…' I look at the stone in her hands, and something tells me it will be all right, that she won't think I'm a loony, that I have to tell her, share with her. 'Sometimes when I hold it, I feel things, see things like…'

'Like wolves…'

I nod and her eyes swallow me, the hill, the sky.

'I don't doubt it, Sam.' She cups the stone, sacred in her palms. 'My grandpa, God rest his soul, would say you were touched by the Fae.'

'The who?'

'It's a Gaelic word, Sam. For the fairies.'

I look into her unblinking gaze, not judging me, or laughing at me. Who is this unknown girl? How does she cast such a spell on me?

'So you don't think I'm imagining it all?'

'No, Sam.' Oona takes off her helmet, and I watch the wind run its fingers through her hair. 'I don't. Here...' Resting the stone in her lap, she takes my hand. 'This is your heart line, Sam. It can tell me a lot of things about you...'

I watch, barely breathing as her finger traces my palm.

'Shouldn't I cross your palm with silver or something?' I laugh, but it doesn't come out right, and all I can do is watch her finger, feel it circle little lines like scars.

'These, here, tell me you've been going through a lot. That you're hurting.'

The wind is picking up, pulling at us. The horses graze. The wolves are gone.

'What else does it tell you?' I move closer, huddle in.

Oona's finger traces the line that stops below my middle finger. She smiles, a secret unlocked.

'That you're the jealous type...'

'Oh dear...'

My hand starts to close over hers, draw her witchy warmth into mine. She looks up as I put my other hand to her freckled face.

'I sound like trouble.'

I can feel her heat, her breath as I lean in.

'Sam...' she whispers my name.

Then slowly, tenderly, wonderfully our lips touch and we kiss.

And I hear those wolves howling in my heart.

Quietly, so quietly I open the kitchen door. It's late and it's dark. From his basket, Alfie thumps his tail, and gives a growl.

'Shhh... It's me, you daft apeth.'

I close the door with a soft *click*.

'Daft what?'

I nearly jump out of my skin. Then I see her, a shadow with Alfie.

'Beth! What are you doing on the floor?'

Her shape merges with his, burying its head.

'Hanging with Alf. And what time do you call this?'

Her phone screen lights, catches her eyes. I remember that look from the other day, mine-sweeping for the truth. My sister who I can't hide from: 'This is me, remember?'

I sit on the floor next to her, my back against a cupboard.

'How's Oona?' she says, swigging from a glass of milk.

I chuckle, because of course Beth knows, and take the glass from her, glugging the cold goodness.

'Terrific. She's… just well, terrific.'

Beth's phone lights again, and I see her wide grin.

'Look at you, the cat that got the…' she takes the glass back, 'milk.'

I reach for Alf's fur, finding Beth's hand in the dark. Her fingers flick mine. My little sister poking me. My little sister tickling me. Far off an owl hoots.

'Remember that time when we camped in the garden?'

Beth grunts. We're both there in the tent, hiding in sleeping bags.

'You were so scared.'

'So were you.'

Her fingers flick mine again.

'Not as much as you.'

'Well, the torch had packed in, hadn't it?'

Beth sniggers. 'You thought Dad outside was a monster.'

I remember the fear running through me, as the zip on the tent slowly opened.

'Yeah, the Thing from the late-night chippy.'

Hello, you two, fancy a midnight feast?

And we're smelling that sharp tang of vinegar.

I got two large bags. Room for one more?

Beth laughs. 'It was such a squeeze.'

'Worth it, though. Best chips ever.'

'Yeah. Best evs.'

We sat in the dark of our tent, me, Beth and Dad, and feasted like kings on those great bags of hot chips that we couldn't see, our hands roaming hungrily for more, as Dad told us stories and made us laugh.

The owl hoots again.

I'm scared of the owl, Dad.

I rest my hand on Beth's.

Ah now, she's only a wise old messenger.

From where, Dad?

We munch down those salty chips, as his voice fills the warm darkness.

Why, from this world to the next.

Beth drains her glass and sighs.

'So what's an apeth?'

My fingers squeeze hers.

'You. You're an apeth.'

Beth moves her tired head to my shoulder.

'Your apeth,' she yawns.

I lean in, as Dad kisses us goodnight and zips us in, safe and sound.

'Yeah,' I whisper.

And from wherever she is in the blue night beyond, the owl calls, as she flies from this world to the next.

'Well, this is a nice way to bunk off school.'

Bill turns to me, grinning that blaze of teeth. 'I don't

see many truant officers making it up here, mind.'

'No.' I smile back at him. 'We'd see them coming.'

'Hold up, lad,' Bill gasps. 'I need a breather.'

I look below us. Walkers are dotted here and there across the curving climb. Bill gazes at the fields stretching into the distance.

'It's not half bad up here, is it? Reckon I can see all the way to Lancashire.'

Badger whines, as the wind ruffles his stippled coat.

'Here, boy!' I toss Alfie's ball up the hill. He tears after it, but the old dog just watches.

'His running days are well over.' Bill leans on his stick. 'Where's this Iron Age fort then, Sam?'

'Not far. Come on.'

Together we climb on, pilgrims on a path. Ahead a group of ramblers, all backpacks and boots. The autumn wind flows over the rise, pulling at Bill's thin hair, and with a last few steps we reach the ridge.

'Would you look at that…'

The old earth ramparts rise, and behind them, the site where the fort once stood at the top of the world. Now there's nothing but grass and sky. And people, like us, who gaze and marvel. How this place stood so long ago, how it saw battles, lives lost and won, how one day it fell and never came back.

'It's so quiet. Peaceful,' says Bill as the wind drops, and we follow the buried spine of the fort. 'It's a beautiful place, lad.'

'Yes,' is all I can say. I shove my hands into my jacket and my thumb jams into the stone.

With my hand around the stone now, I search for him. That tall man, striding. But I see no ancient god, no wolves or ravens. Perhaps there never was. But then I think of Oona, that light of knowing in her dark eyes.

The witches used them in their magick.

I think of her lips, of how I want to kiss them again and again, fall deep under her spell.

We move through a ditch in the earthworks, leaving the safety of the fort, and the wind pounces, pressing our cheeks, blowing into our ears.

The ramblers are taking photos. As we make the edge of the rise, I catch that spur of white chalk.

'There...' I point down. 'There's the head. And there...' I point again. 'There's a leg. See? Like it's leaping.'

Bill nods. 'I see it, Sam. That's a wonder of the world, and no mistake.' He glances into the sky. 'Reckon those birds get a better view, though.'

My hand turns the stone.

'That's what Dad used to say...'

But I do not see him here either. Now doubt creeps into my heart that I ever did.

'Hey, lad, you're shaking...' He clasps my shoulder. 'Are you cold?'

I shake my head. I just need to ride it out, being here, at our place without Dad.

'You know...' Bill clears his throat, 'I keep making

cups of tea for May.' He watches a seagull calling in the huge sky. 'I miss her so much, that I don't know what to do with myself.'

My arm won't stop shaking. Bill reaches to stop it.

'Hey, you'll shake yourself to pieces if you don't...'

I take the stone out my pocket. For a moment, I get the feeling that I'm showing him an animal, something alive.

'Where did you get that, Sam?' Bill looks down at the white stone, flecks of light catching the sun.

'Found it. Not far from here. There's a dead tree... Oona called it a scrying stone.'

'Oona, eh?' Bill licks his chapped lips. 'Sounds like that lass has witching ways.'

It makes me start, Bill saying that. Oona's book on dowsing, that story about the burn on her mother's hands. Her fortune-telling finger teasing my palm.

The wind blows through long grass, and the stone turns.

Turns and turns and turns.

A voice close behind me.
'She is everywhere.'

And there on the hillside, are the two girls.

I dare not breathe as I watch them. The older one is crying.

'Wherever we go, she is with us and she sees us.'

The younger strokes her sister's red hair, and pulls her along.

'So I do not want you a sad sister, Evey. And Mother would not want that neither.'

She waggles a thin finger and it makes her sister laugh.

The stone turns in my hand, and the vision changes.

They are holding hands, looking out across the land.

'Let us go,' says Evey.

'Ah, Evey!' cries the younger one. *'You are the best sister! The very best I know!'*

They jump into the sunlight, dancing into the wind. And they're gone.

'You all right, lad?' Bill is watching me carefully. 'You look a bit peaky.'

I nod. What I just saw – between those girls – was so full of love. They had lost someone, but they had each other. But who were they? Why was the stone showing me this? And was it only me?

Without meaning to, the words come out,

'Would you... would you like to hold it?'

He reaches slowly to lift the stone from my hands.

'It's... cold, like ice. Strange – you'd think it'd be warm from your hands.'

I think about others' hands. Witches' hands. Oona's hands.

'Do you see anything, Bill?'

'I see a daft apeth.'

'Seriously, though. Do you see two girls? One red-haired, one smaller and dark?'

'Nowt, Sam.' Bill shakes his head. 'But then perhaps I'm not looking for something, like you seem to be.'

I don't know how this stone works. But it's showing me things, and only me. When I fought Dan's pack, it made me strong and fast. When I saw Dad that first time. The girls and Odin. They were all there, flash after flash.

'Oona said that witches used scrying stones to open other worlds,' I say, aloud. 'So what if... What if I could use this in some way?'

'How do you mean, lad?'

Can't believe I'm saying this, but the ideas are coming now.

'I could reach him. My dad. Talk to him?'

Bill pulls on Badger's fur and sighs again.

'You're off your rocker…'

'It's too busy up here today, that's it.' I point at the groups of people. 'I'll come back, when I can focus.'

'I'm no witch, lad.' Bill pulls Badger. 'But I reckon things like that…' he points at the stone, 'can draw trouble.'

'You think it's dangerous?'

'I think people can be dangerous.' He hooks Badger's lead. 'So in the wrong hands, anything can happen.'

I look at the stone, primed to explode. Oona's lilting words whisper close,

Touched by the Fae.

'So what – I'm dangerous, Bill?'

The wind whips and the sky darkens. Right on cue. He starts to limp down the hill, pulling the old dog behind him

'Only if you want to be, lad. Only if you want to be.'

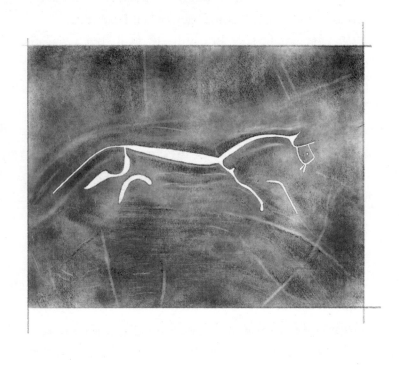

I'm pouring tea when Mum comes in.

We both smile knowingly at each other, because of the story she's told me so many times. Of how Gran would appear for a cup, just as Mum thought of filling the kettle: 'She'd read the tea leaves before they were brewed!'

So I pour a big mug and hand it to her, watching her wedding ring clink the china.

'So where have you been, love?'

'The White Horse with —'

I hesitate. I don't want to tell her about Bill and the stone.

'... with Chad.'

Mum takes a swig of her tea, muttering, 'Maybe this should be something stronger...' Then she puts the cup down hard, making me jump. From his basket, Alfie barks.

'Mum?'

'Can I ask you not to lie to me, Sam?'

'What... do you mean?'

She rubs her head.

'I know this is hard. God knows, I know. You're out all the time, back late at night and I can take that, because I know you've got to do what you've got to do... But...'

Her arms stretch across the table to me. I'm frozen, aware of the tension rising in her.

'But, love – Chad called round here this evening looking for you...'

It feels like a glass of water has been tipped down my neck. I'm an idiot. Should have told Chad to cover for me.

'I... I...' But I've got nothing, and Mum knows it. She raises a hand.

'He came here after school, who phoned me today because you've not been in for a while.'

Another glass of water down my back.

'They said it's fine. They said you need time. Which, of course, you do.'

'Mum, I was—'

'Just listen to me, Sam. I'm not interested in school. I need to get this all out...'

She picks up the teapot and pours another cup.

'It's your business, Sam, and I'm not going to pry into who you're hanging out with. But, please. Please don't lie to me.'

I glug quickly, feeling her eyes on me.

'It's just us now, Sam. Me and you and Beth. So don't bring lies between us, that's all I ask. Okay?'

I swallow the tea held in my mouth. No sugar.

'Okay, Mum.'

Her shoulders drop. I reach across the table and feel for her hand. It's cold as always. She always has cold hands. Dad called her his Vampire Queen.

'Sam, there's another thing. I've been trying to talk to you about it.'

Oh no. Not this. Not now. But there's nowhere to run.

'I want you to make your peace with Dad.'

I reach for my cup. It's empty.

Her cold grip tightens, as Dad whispers, *The Vampire Queen has you in her clutches.*

'Sam?'

'I… I have.' Another lie. And she knows it. We both do.

'Love, you know you haven't – you need to talk about what happened.'

'When?'

She sighs. 'You know when, Sam. The night before he died.'

Yes. I do know. Of course I know. It's the thing I can never undo.

'You need to talk about what happened between you.'

'What good would talking about it do?'

Mum stiffens.

'Because you're carrying it with you.'

Now it's my turn to shrug.

'Well, life's tough, isn't it?'

'Yes, it is. But it's tough enough without the guilt I know you're feeling.'

I can't sit here anymore. I stand and go to fill the kettle. My hands shake under the tap.

'I hoped… and I don't want to pry, Sam—'

'But you're going to anyway, right?'

I bite down, trapping the sarcasm that hisses out of me. Mum's standing too. She moves to my shoulder.

'I hoped that doctor would help.'

'Mum, she *is* helping.'

I feel her stroke my shoulder. I will not cry. I will not.

'If you can't talk to me about it, I hope you can talk to her?'

Her hands still. Waiting for an answer.

'Is this your idea of client-doctor confidentiality?'

The sarcasm wriggles free.

'Just promise me you'll try, will you? For me? Please…'

I can hear the strain in her voice, as if she's holding a hundred planets.

'I pro—'

My phone buzzes. Thank Christ. Chad, Oona, anyone! I pull my phone out.

It's a number I don't recognise. And that's enough to make my belly churn, as I read the words on the screen.

Hope you're going to the party, Sammy boy.

I freeze as I watch another little chat bubble appear.

Now I have your number, we can stay in touch…

Mum's humming into my back, as another chat bubble lifts to show someone out there in the dark of the night is talking to me right now.

Like old friends…

A picture appears. It's a clod of mud in someone's hand.

'You've got some odd friends, Sam.' The hairs on my neck rise as Mum looks over my shoulder. 'Why would they send you that?'

Something thuds against the kitchen window. A picture leaning against it slides to the floor, glass cracking. Alfie starts barking his head off.

'What in heaven's name—?'

Mum flings open the back door. More mud hits the window.

'Get out of it, you little beggars!'

Laughter and hooting. Mum steps out shaking her fist.

'Clear off before I call the police!'

Jeers as they sprint away. Shapes with hoods. Shapes I know.

I'm breathing rapidly as I hold Mum, as I look down at the broken picture of Dad. The one of him in his uniform, a splinter of glass through his grin.

'Look at that! Look at what those beggars have done! Look at what they did!'

Mum's furious but there's fear in her voice too.

'Who would do such a thing, Sam? Who would do that?'

'I don't know, Mum…' I lie, already breaking my promise to my mother, looking at my fallen father. 'I don't know.'

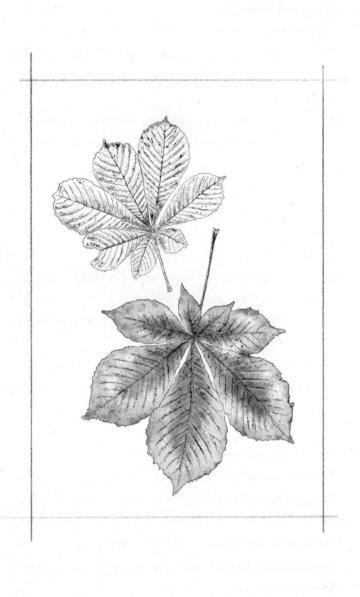

I t's cold. I push open the clinic door, glad of the warm blast that welcomes me.

My phone buzzes. Chad.

Dan McGuire. The Grudge, they should call him.

I picture Dan, grinning oafishly as he lobbed mud at our kitchen window.

You going to tell the police?

Mum has. For what it's worth.

Can I help?

Doubt it.

Mate, all those years ago, with Dan. I owe you.

I change the subject.

You coming on Saturday?

The Halloween Party beckoned. I think about Oona's freckled smile, that glint of her dark eyes.

Yes. Hope so. You?

Yeah. Gotta date?

I think about her lips whispering my name.

Yes, Oona! You?

Chad's chat bubble hovers. Chad a date? How many dates more like.

That's great, mate! Yeah, think so…

He thinks so! Another bubble…

Remember it's fancy dress, monkey man.

At last year's party Chad and I hired gorilla suits. Hot as hell, but such a laugh.

Gotta go, I'm late.

Chad sends a thumbs-up and a gorilla emoji.

I know the costume I want, the only thing I want to wear. I wonder about checking my size with the rental place when Rachel opens her office door.

'Sam. Good to see you.'

She smiles, her grey gaze calm and steady.

'Hi there.'

As I sit in the armchair, it feels like ages since I was here. But there's still the shadow of a bruise on my hand, a reminder of the fight and running through the rain. So much has happened since then. Now I have a date with Oona.

'You seem happy, Sam. Has something happened?'

A cup of tea sits on the little table. Steam curls in the light from the window.

'There's a party this Saturday.'

Already I can taste the smoke from flares and hear the thrum of the bass through my feet. I can see myself and Oona dancing and laughing. There's Chad with his mystery date, and all my other mates from school.

'I can tell you're looking forward to it,' Rachel laughs.

'Yeah.' I nod. 'Yeah, I am.'

'Good.' She looks at her pad. Notes already, or were they there before?

'How's the hand?' Rachel points at my tell-tale knuckles.

'Oh… okay, thanks.'

I shove my hand into my jacket. A sure-fire signal that I have something to hide. And, of course, that hiding thing, the stone, meets my fingers.

'Bill and you seem to be getting on well. Have you seen him again?'

I turn the stone, thinking of it in Bill's gnarled hand, as he searched for spirits, thinking about what he said.

I'm not looking for something, like you seem to be.

'No…' I say.

How can I tell her that I'm trying to convince him of the powers of the stone to conjure my dad from another place, and how I thought we could try again? I have to change the subject. I know what I have to do. Frying pan to the fire.

'Before you said… that I could talk about anything I wanted.'

'Yes, Sam. These are your sessions.' Rachel puts down her cup, and outside the wind rustles the horse chestnut leaves. 'We can go anywhere you like.'

I look at its thick black trunk beneath that swirl of

orange. If I could go anywhere, it would be to the desert that took Dad. Before the bomb that blew us apart. But things like that aren't possible. So we're stuck, pinned in time.

'The night before... before...' I trip over my words. Rachel holds that calm gaze of hers as I take a breath and start again.

'The night before Dad died, we had a video call...'

The tree sways. I can see our kitchen, the laptop on the table. I can see Dad's grainy face on the screen. Mum and Beth are there, and I'm at the back door. My heart beats fast from running.

'Was there something different about this call, Sam?'

I look across the kitchen. Rachel's standing in the corner. Dad's face buffers.

'We'd already heard he was going to be another two months on the tour... something about another battalion redeployed. I don't know. But it felt like another lifetime.'

Dad's grin, frozen on screen.

'I was late. Mum was really cross.'

I look at her, looking really cross at me. And I was really cross too. A few of us had met up in the park. Chad with Chloe, Darren and Tash. Even moody Gina was being nice for a change. We were having a laugh. And then Mum started calling and texting, and she wouldn't let up: *Sam, come home NOW! Your dad's on the laptop!*

Even her way of saying it made me cross, as if he was on TV or something. I look at Rachel, observing us.

'I mean, what was there to talk about? He wasn't coming home, did we have to wallow in it?' I step into the kitchen. 'And of course Beth was being peacemaker, but I was spoiling for a fight. Mum calling me home like I was ten years old or something!'

I feel my hand clench the stone.

Seeing Beth make space on her chair, beckoning me, trying to dampen the fire. She knew, she saw the anger boiling inside me.

'Hey, Sammy! How was your night?'

Rachel and I turn at the sound of my dad's voice. His smile fills the screen, warm and broad as ever. He's so pleased to see me, but something in me doesn't want to play. *Sammy*. He's called me that ever since I was little. Most times I like it, because it's his name for me, even though I'm almost as big as him. But now, I hate it. Especially now.

'It *was* great. It *was* fun. And *now* it's over.'

'Oh…' Dad's smile falters. 'I'm sorry, son. You didn't have to—'

'Sam needed to be home anyway, Alan,' Mum butts in, full of frowns.

My cheeks burn. Treating me like a kid. 'I didn't need to be here—'

'You do with your dad wanting to talk to you.'

'Sheila, hush now.' Dad's picture judders and jumps. 'Sam, it wasn't for anything special. Just nice to see—'

'Not a single reply to my messages.' Mum glares, not

letting it go. 'So rude!'

'Sheila...'

'Mum—' Beth leans between us. But the fire jumps in me and I let it rage.

'Messages! That's a joke. Orders more like.'

'I beg your pardon?'

'You heard,' I snap.

Mum seethes, 'Then hear this—!'

'PLEASE!'

The laptop crackles. We all look at Dad.

'Please don't argue. Please stop...' He reaches to the side of the screen, as though he's trying to touch us. I can almost feel his fingers brush my hot cheeks.

I miss him. I miss him. I miss him.

No. Something in me turns, something that's stupid and selfish. I didn't mean to say it. It just left my mouth.

'Why? Why do you care, Dad?'

The fire grows and grows in my belly, wanting to burn and destroy.

'Sam, I do care.' He comes closer to the screen. 'So very much.'

'Ha!' I spit, feeling Beth's hand on my arm. Not this time, Bethy. 'If you... if you cared so much about us, you wouldn't be out in that sodding desert!'

'Sam!' Mum pulls at me. She can pull all she likes.

'It's the last tour, Sam. When we're done, that's it—'

'Yeah, right!'

'Sammy...'

'Stop calling me that!' I stand fast, stumbling away from kind Dad, from cross Mum, from peacemaker Beth.

Dad's face hasn't frozen. He's just still and quiet is all. So still and quiet as he says, 'Sam, I will come back to you.'

Mum has started to cry and Beth holds her, as Rachel watches us. A real family. Good Beth. Bad Sam.

'And we'll walk to the White Horse together, eh?' He smiles. 'I promise, Sam.'

My fists clench. I want to smash something.

'I don't want your promises.'

'Oh, Sam,' Mum sobs. 'Oh, Sam, please...'

'I know, I know,' Dad whispers. 'It's all I have, son. I'm sorry.'

His smile is so warm, so understanding, so my dad who I love and who isn't here. I nearly pick the laptop up and smash it against the wall.

'I don't want your sorries, either.'

I look at them, my family, but none of them speak. The fire flashes from me, burns them all good and proper.

'Just stay there, Dad, since you love it so much...'

'I don't. I love you, Sam.' His face, his voice so far away. 'More than salt.'

Now it's my turn to tremble and that makes me crosser than anything. I don't want him to see me like this, to see me afraid. So through a mist of tears I say, 'If you loved me, you'd be here, you'd find some way...'

He nods, whispering, 'Okay, Sammy, I will.'

'Stop it! I told you—' I choke, forcing the words out. 'Don't call me that.'

'I'm sorr —'

'Oh, sorry again?' I can't look at him. Only shout. 'Just stay there, Dad. Stay in the desert for ever!'

I turn and run from the kitchen. I don't care.

'Sam!' Beth calls, but I've already gone.

To find my friends, to hate my dad.

And I did. All night long.

The branches bend, snared by the wind that catches and tumbles my family's faces, scattered in the leaves.

'That was the last time you spoke to your father, wasn't it, Sam?'

My fingernail worries that notch on the stone, picking, picking. My throat aches from talking.

Rachel leans forward, so I have to look at her.

'Sam, these feelings. That your father wasn't coming home. That you were having fun with you friends... you feel guilty, but there's nothing to blame yourself for.'

I hold her gaze. 'I damned him to that desert.'

Rachel puts down her pen. 'Do you really believe that? That you cursed him?'

I stare at her, but it's me that blinks first.

And something comes to me, sung by two dancing

girls upon a hill. An idea that hatches in my mind, as a bird freed from its egg.

'Perhaps I can find him again.' It's got to work, it just has to.

The stone sits cupped in Oona's hands.

'To tell the future, to read the past… to open other worlds.'

Dad stands beneath the gaze of a god who gathers the dead.

Sam, I will come back to you.

'What do you mean by that, Sam?' I can barely hear Rachel above the threshing leaves.

I'm standing, moving through time and space, far away to where the White Horse leaps across the land.

'I know what to do now. Thank you, Rachel.'

'Sam, wait! What? What *are* you going to do?'

My hand curves around the stone, the key that's always been there.

'Find a witch, of course.'

II ⊙ THE HIGH PRIESTESS

Mrs Pratt turns in surprise as I tap on the glass. She puts down her book, unusual for her, and comes towards us.

'Love Mrs Pratt...' Oona waves. 'Let's hope she's in a good mood.'

'She's always in a good mood,' I say, as our school librarian opens the back doors onto the playing fields. Leaves scuttle into the warmth. I breath in that lovely papery smell.

'Sam and Oona – I can't say it's not nice to see you...' Mrs Pratt does her thing of looking over her half glasses. 'But it is the half term break, as I'm sure you're aware, and, well... I was rather hoping to catch up on admin during the supposed peace and quiet.'

'We're really sorry to disturb you, Mrs Pratt...' I glance at Oona, who nods. 'But would it be okay to look a few things up? We'll be quick —'

'And quiet,' Oona nudges me, 'as church mice.'

'As the grave,' I add. Oona stifles a giggle.

Mrs Pratt sighs. 'If you two weren't among my most dedicated readers, it would be a resounding "get thee gone"... but I am prepared to make an exception.' She bars the way. 'The price of entry, however, is a packet of ginger nuts on your return to studies. Do you accept these onerous terms?' She gives a haughty glare, her thin frame becoming taller.

'We do!' Oona and I laugh together.

'Then welcome, young explorers, to my blessed hall of wisdom.' Mrs Pratt bows and ushers us into her domain.

'We really appreciate it, Mrs Pratt,' says Oona, as I walk ahead, studying the dark rows of slumbering books. 'Can I ask if that book I ordered has come in, please?'

Mrs Pratt reaches behind her desk to a pile of books, all tongues of white paper.

'You are quite the devourer of divination, Oona.' She holds up the book, an illustration of brightly coloured cards on its cover. 'Last month it was a guide to dowsing and now...' she peers at the cover, '*Tarot: Turning to the Future*. Perhaps you might tell my fortune one of these days?'

Oona blushes and tucks the book under her arm.

'It would be my absolute pleasure, Mrs Pratt. Could you point us in the direction of Local History?'

'Third aisle on the left, History and Folklore. Now, I don't want to hear a peep from you two. Or else you can do my filing.'

Mrs Pratt, the best librarian there is, shoos us away.

'Hey, can I see?'

I tug the tarot book from Oona, and flick through its pages: each spread has a picture of a card. The illustrations are strange and so detailed. Medieval figures pose among symbols and objects, some with weird titles. 'The Hermit.' 'The High Priestess.'

'What's a… "Page of Cups?"'

Oona is a few steps away, searching through the books.

'Pages were messengers for the courts of the old kings and queens.'

The card shows a young man or a woman, dressed in a tunic and long scarf, kind of like a Shakespearean actor. They're standing on a seashore, a golden cup in their hand. There's something dreamlike about the picture – I think I've seen it before, but can't remember where.

'The card is about youth. The child you once were.'

Oona's voice drifts down the aisle, circling me, as I gaze into the picture.

'It's about listening to the messages of your past to know your future.'

Then I notice something. Was it there before?

'There's a fish in his cup!' I smile, as Oona turns the cracked, yellowing pages of a hefty tome, her black eyes dancing.

'It represents surprise, Sam…'

The fish and the page are looking at each other. Every time I look at this picture, it seems there are new things to be found, as if I'm being drawn into a little world.

'It means to expect the unexpected.'

I quiver at her words caressing my spine, conjuring the feeling of someone there, standing in the shadows. But there's only Oona peering at a book that's opened right from my memory.

'Are you all right, Sam? You look like you've seen a ghost.'

'Not a ghost...' I say. 'My dad gave me this same book once as a present...'

I'm twelve again and my hands smooth the snarling silver dragon on its cover.

'*Norse Myths and Legends...*' Mum had whispered. Yet now it's Oona leaning closer to read, as the pages fall inevitably to that picture I have looked at so many times, drifting to sleep, where a god would wake and step into my dreams.

'Odin,' Oona reads as Dad had read beside me, his stubble on my cheek. 'He walked the vale with his wild hunt, leading the fallen to his great hall...'

I hear my voice, but it doesn't sound like my own. 'I remember Beth saying, "Is he your favourite god, Daddy?" And how he loved that.'

Oona's finger traces Odin's tall frame, past the patch on his eye, down a great staff, to rest upon the head of a wolf.

'Wolves...' she says.

I feel the weight of the stone in my pocket. I dare not

touch it. Odin gazes out and I remember. Falling into whiteness. My head splitting.

'Oona,' I pull back, as though I'm on a cliff top, 'can we look at something else?'

'Surely, Sam.' She closes the book away, and moves further down the aisle, smoothing the books, as if she's sensing the murmur of buried stories.

And for a while – I don't know how long – we move silently through pages, across maps and guides, in and out of pictures, photographs, stepping through an avenue of words, until we're in a small section, where the books look ancient, as if they're carved out of tree trunks. I watch Oona drawn towards them, eyes glinting at their old spines, until finally she nods and reaches for her find. It's as if she's coaxing a creature out of its burrow.

'Here now, could this be what we're looking for... A history of local folklore...?' Oona opens the volume, and turns its creaking, cracking pages of old woodcuts, devils and fire, black cats and broomsticks.

'There's a story about a witch trial near here, led by a witchfinder called Matthew Jacobs. He had it in for healers and old women who could cure toothache with the right herbs.' Again her fingers move across the page, almost as though she is absorbing something from the image of a row of miserable women, nooses about their necks. A man in a tall hat points at them. He's smiling. Oona isn't.

'But seems it didn't go to plan...' She turns the page

and bends to read aloud, her head almost touching mine. '"*Two true witches did battle and save those ill-fortuned women. Many fell upon that Day of the Witches.*" Here they are, don't they look bad ass?'

I stare at the woodcut and my breath catches. There's a little girl with a thatch of hair like a crow's nest. She's holding hands with an older girl, a slash of a frown on her brow. They're standing on a hill. No, they're dancing.

'Sam… look at her hand.'

I do a double take and my stomach clenches.

'She's holding a stone…'

Oona looks at me. 'Or *the* stone? Didn't you say you found it nearby?'

I stare back at her, thinking of that day. The flashes, lightning in my mind. When I saw those unknown girls. Then Dad. Then Odin.

Oona's body is so close to mine as she reads. I feel my cheeks burn, I want to touch her.

'There was a great battle over the stone – the elder sister and another, a dark witch…' her eyes dart across the page, 'who died up on the hills during a terrible storm…' She pauses. 'Legend says that on All Hallow's Eve, you can still see the sisters trying to find their way home…'

All Hallow's Eve. Halloween.

'But we know it as Samhain, don't we, Sam?' Oona reads my thoughts as if they'd fallen upon the open book. 'And didn't your father?' She raises an eyebrow. It's as if she's drawing something from me. I look from her to those black dancing figures. Witches circling me.

'What does it mean…?'

The library is silent. Only the books can hear us breathe.

Gently, Oona picks up the tarot book, and closing her eyes, she begins to flick through the pages.

'Tell me when to stop.'

Flick, flick, flick and she's a blur, a spirit of the book.

'Stop,' I say and she does instantly.

Without opening her eyes, she turns the page towards me.

'What do you see?'

'There's a guy floating in the clouds. And a couple. They're naked in front of a tall hill,' I whisper.

Oona opens her eyes.

'It's a card about communication, Sam… This fellow in the cloud is the angel, Raphael, whose name means "God heals". See how the man looks at the woman, who looks at the angel…'

I look too, and as before, new things seem to appear, a tableau unfurling.

'… they show a connection, a path.'

'To where?' I put my hand on the book, my fingers edging hers.

'To who you want to be.' Her finger rests between the figures, who I realise are Adam and Eve in the garden. 'To the naked truth of yourself.'

I move my hand over Oona's.

'And the card,' I whisper. 'It's called 'The Lovers'...'

She watches me stroke her fingers, so gently, so slowly.

She smiles and I yearn for her.

Oona puts her other hand on mine, gives it a gentle shake.

'We have things to do, Sam.' She raises those dark eyes to mine. 'Magick things.'

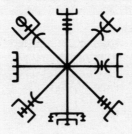

Three weeks since we buried you.

You taught me how to play chess.

You taught me about the birds.

You taught me your magic trick, of how to pull off my thumb.

You taught me how to bowl a cricket ball, how to ride a bike.

You taught me to look after Beth, be there for Mum.

You taught me life's for living.

You taught me well.

PAGE OF CUPS

B ill's car pulls into the White Horse car park, its headlights sweeping the empty spaces. A fox turns towards us, eyes catching like flames.

'Oh dear.' Bill pulls the handbrake. 'We've disturbed her hunt.'

The vixen pads past, head low, her coat gleaming gold.

'Isn't she a wonder of nature?'

Her white-tipped tail slips between the bushes. Then, after a moment, the gorse shakes, and a figure steps into the light.

'Well, now...' Bill reaches for his tartan bag. 'Seems your Oona is a shape-shifter.'

I look out at her, shielding her eyes from the headlights.

'She's not *mine*, Bill. She's just...' I struggle to find words, because of course, there's nothing I want more. 'Just Oona, all right?'

Bill can see me squirm, he nods, all serious, and cuts the ignition.

'Fair enough, lad.' He pats my arm, as if to say, You're totally gone, down the rabbit hole, lost in her Wonderland. 'Well, you talked me into this, so are you ready, Sam?'

I peer up at the leaden sky. A seam of light on the horizon means dawn isn't far. I feel the lump of the stone nudging my side. I sense the gaze of my waiting friends, Oona the shape-shifter, Bill clinging on to that old bag of his. I know their bellies buzz like mine.

'Ready, Bill.'

The hill looms. We follow the beams of our torches bouncing off the mist. It's as though we're mountaineers edging towards base camp, and beneath us the land is shrouded in a blanket of grey.

'Pleased to meet you at last, Oona – parky, ain't it?' Bill pulls his coat around him.

'Pleased to meet you at last too, Bill,' she says and steers him shy of a rock slick with dew. 'You should feel the west of Ireland in winter.'

'The West Coast, eh? I know my accents. Let me see…' Bill cocks a wizened finger, an old professor plucking inspiration from the cold air. 'You're from… Cork.'

'I am not!' Oona shakes her head.

'Dingle, then?'

She chuckles. 'Get out of it. I'll give you one more try – don't blow it.'

Bill grins. How quickly my friends have become friends. I would feel jealous if I didn't like watching them tease and laugh.

'I've got it—' Bill clasps her arm. 'Kerry! You're a Kerry girl!'

She fixes him with a look that takes no prisoners.

'I am a *lady* of Connemara, Bill – and don't you ever forget it.'

He touches his forelock, and I think of the Page of Cups, bowing to his queen.

'Look, the path…'

Our lights find the white chalk and we climb on through the chill. It's quiet, but for our breathing. Nothing stirs, no birds cry. Not even any wind. And I'm wondering how far to go, when the ground rises sharply, and a long bank appears out of the fog. The old ramparts.

'The fort's ahead, come on…'

We move forward, eager to reach that wide open space beyond the earthworks.

'Here…' I guide Bill and Oona through a gap in the mound of grass, then I hurry on into the murk, the wet grass soaking my boots. And I feel that familiar pull, that I've had ever since I was little, the urge to race across the plain, pushing through the bustle of the castle all around me.

'Hold up, Sam!'

Bill's torch searches the mist and I stop. The ramparts curl about, like the shadow of a slumbering serpent. Our breath clouds and I think about me and Beth in the snow, pretending to be dragons, roaring smoke into the air.

'Nice to be ahead of the crowds, eh, lad?'

'Yeah...'

Then we both look at Oona stepping before us, a priestess ready for ceremony.

She turns off her torch. Without a word, Bill and I do the same. It's funny. Feels more respectful somehow, like whispering in a church. In the deafening silence, we watch a sliver of dawn, new life edging the darkness.

'Sam?'

Oona's voice makes me jump.

'The stone...'

'Oh, yeah, of course...'

I reach into my pocket, delving into a warm nest, to draw the sleeping stone, ice cold as always, into the open. It stares at us, an eye in my palm.

'What...?' Bill clears his throat. 'What happens now, lass?' His lips quiver with the cold.

Oona takes my hand, then Bill's. My chest fills to feel her soft warmth, and I fight to stop my thumb from stroking hers.

'I will connect our circle...' Her voice lilts in the clammy air. 'With the stone joined between you and Sam.'

Bill looks at my other hand, and the thing that waits and watches.

'Like a séance, you mean...'

Oona looks at him, that same steady gaze with eyes as deep as space.

'There are many words for it. To open a door. The Latin Americans called it "misa", and the Ancient Greeks "necromancy".' She smiles. 'On the West Coast, we call it simply "Echtra" – an outing to the Otherworld.'

Bill blinks and I want to laugh, because I know what's racing through his mind about this lady of Connemara, wise before her time, as if she's been here before – been here always.

'Right you are, Oona lass...' he whispers. Carefully, as though he's testing hot water, Bill reaches his other wrinkled hand to close it around mine, around the stone.

'Good...' Oona nods and the mist seems to swirl nearer, breathing, listening. 'Now Bill, Sam, close your eyes...'

Bill gives a shaky smile and clears his throat. He closes his eyes.

I breathe deep, before I do the same and fall into darkness, where there is only Oona's voice.

'... and think on them. The ones you have lost...'

Her words, a sacred song I never want to end.

'Think, with all your will...'

So I do, feeling the cold on my cheeks.

The weight of the stone, Bill's hand in mine.

'With all your love...'

I know you're there. I know you can hear me.

'Think on them...'

The silence grows.

And grows.

And grows.

Bill's fingers twitch with mine.

A bird cries.

Too sharp for a gull.

Too low for a skylark.

It cries again. Close by. A flurry of wings. And I know what it is.

An owl.

I remember the wind on my body. The stone against my brow. Hurtling through the clouds.

Another cry. No. A voice.

'*... this way, Evey!*'

'*Dill!*'

Two voices.

I open my eyes to see Bill and Oona, wide-eyed like me, listening like me.

'*... slow down, silly mite!*'

Because we can all hear what we should not be hearing.

'*But I'm excited, Evey. Aren't you?*'

It's a girl's voice, clear as anything, and the hairs on my neck rise.

'*About what, Dill?*'

And I turn my head so slowly to see what we all see. Two figures parting the mist.

'*Samhain, silly Evey Bird.*'

Two girls stepping barefoot through the wet grass. One is small and thin, hair black as pitch. The other older, fox red, a frown fixed firmly on her face. Those unknown girls I saw when I first held the stone, *their* scrying stone. The girls from the book in the library, *two true witches*, have leaped from its pages, danced out of time.

'*Isn't it always Samhain with you?*' The older girl wraps her arm around her sister. '*For the feasting and the dancing most likes...*'

They pass across the plain, skirts switching, and with a gasp, I realise that they can't see us.

'*No, Evey.*' The girl Dill plucks a blade of grass. '*Samhain is when our world touches other worlds...*' She stops and looks our way, and our breath holds as one, '*when the paths are open.*'

She smiles.

'*...when the spirits walk.*'

'*Then walk faster, little spirit of mine,*' her sister calls her on. '*We have a way to go...*'

The little girl blows hard through the grass, making a shrill, echoing whistle. Then with a last look back, she turns and follows her sister into the mist.

'By heck…' I feel the jolt through our circle of hands, as Bill tries to pull away.

'Wait…' Oona whispers.

Our hearts beat in our throats, because something is padding towards us with a whine, and fast-paced paws.

A wolf, black and burly, lopes across the plain. It waits, whining, as another pants from the fog. Their eyes roam and I feel Oona's hand shake, so I grip it tighter, as we watch the wolves sniff, looking about expectantly. They give a low howl and their ears prick.

Because now there's a figure walking the ramparts. Tall and bearded, it raises a staff in the soupy air where we can just make out ravens swooping. The wolves streak to their master, their god of the dead, as he strides below the ridge, and drifts into grey nothing.

The mist moves.

I hear a laugh. For a moment I think the little girl has returned to pluck more grass. But as two more figures step along the ramparts, I know it's not her.

'Dad! It's Halloween tomorrow! Halloween!'

It's me.

'Samhain I call it…'

And my dad.

'… when —'

'When our world and the spirit world meet, I know, Dad, you've said it a million times.'

'Hey, look.' He points ahead through the mist of my memory. *'See that man up there – do you see?'*

'*Yeah, Dad,*' I cry out, my voice echoing through the years. '*He's got such big dogs...*'

'*And birds too.*' Dad waves. '*He's waving, Sam.*'

The tears run free, as I watch Dad wave, wave, wave, and then we fade, folded into time.

The mist shivers. Like us.

It's over.

Somewhere in the lightening clouds, there comes a long, low cry.

The owl swoops over us and is gone.

197

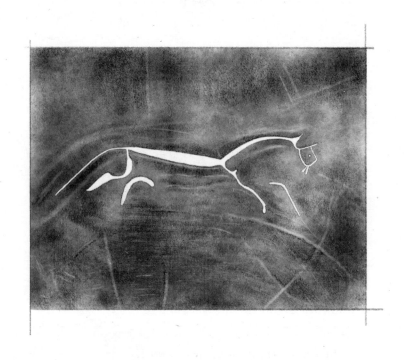

The journey back from the White Horse has been quiet. Sunlight cuts through the empty trees. The shadows of the clouds race across the valley in the early morning. It's as if the mist was never here.

But it was, we all were and we all saw what we saw.

From the passenger seat, Oona looks from me to Bill, who drives as if he's in a trance.

'Are you two all right?'

The car radio is murmuring classical music, the soundtrack to our thoughts.

'I am…' I nod. I feel as if I've just woken up. 'Bill…?'

'Oh, I'm all right.' He tries to smile. 'I'm just worried you know… Not like that – for Badger, he'll have the right hump. You don't know what he's like…' He starts to joke, then stops. I know he wants to say more about what happened, but then I also know we're all turning it over, as if we're sifting a jigsaw for the right pieces.

'That was some show, Oona,' I say, feeling the press of

the stone at my side, so full of secrets.

'Yes…' Brightness dapples her freckled face. 'It showed a lot.'

'What do you mean?'

'Get over, will you…' Bill mutters. There's another car ahead, stationary in the road.

Oona turns. 'Don't you see, Sam?'

Bill beeps the horn, and hauls on the steering wheel.

'Sam—' Oona pulls my arm, she's shaking me. 'The witches, you and your dad …'

We're passing the car, plumes of vape swirling from its half-opened windows.

'… they were about Samhain, Halloween. About tomorrow night.'

Something stirs in me, a key turning, as I watch a tinted window wind down, and a bearded face blows smoke like a dragon and grins, baring its big teeth.

'Sammy boy!'

A dragon called Dan McGuire.

'Bill, get a move on.'

'What's that?' He glances around, as we start to pick up speed. 'Just a bunch of idiots, lad…'

Idiots I know too well.

A horn blares. Dan's car is bombing up, lights flashing.

'What the…?' Bill yells. 'Get out of it, you maniacs!'

But they're on us, swerving and blaring, and as I watch dry-mouthed, my fingers clamped to the seat, Dan leans out, giving the finger, shouting against the wind,

'Next time I see you, Sammy boy. I'll give you a flamin' stone!'

'Bill!' Oona shouts. A lorry, coming fast on the other side of the road. My guts turn to water.

Wheels shriek. Dan's car cuts across us. The lorry skids and skids.

Bill hits the brakes, the car twists, we slam forward.

'Bill?' Oona reaches over. 'Bill, are you all right?'

He's white and shaking. A bruise spreads on his temple.

'Maniacs. Could have… killed us…'

I'm shaking too, remembering Dan's grin. I could kill him.

'I'm calling the police…' Oona reaches for her phone.

'No, lass…'

'But they can't get away with that…'

'Please, lass. No trouble…'

I finally find words. 'Bill, that guy, I know him.'

'From the park, aye. Looks like we all know him now, eh?'

This is down to me. If I hadn't started things with Dan, this would never have happened.

'Bill, I'm sorry – I —'

He grips my wrist.

'Don't be soft.' He turns back to the wheel and puts his shocked little car into gear, and we lurch away, numb and dumb.

Through the lace curtains at Bill's kitchen window I watch a robin dart about his garden domain. It hops and stops, then looks bravely back at me.

Bill sits at a table, a mug of tea in his hands. There's a blob of arnica on his forehead, from a kit Oona found. Badger sighs, resting his big head on his master's knee. He knows something isn't right.

'Do you need some painkillers, Bill?' Oona asks.

'No. No, thank you, lass,' he says quietly, stroking the old dog.

'Another cup of tea?'

He shakes his head. He looks spent.

'Well, can I get—?'

'I don't need anything, Sam. Thank you all the same.'

I sweep up his mug, my nerves jangling as I rinse it. There's a picture on the windowsill. Bill with his arm around May. They're laughing. I wonder what made them giggle like that. I wonder what Bill thinks every time he stands at this sink alone.

'You know, back there on the hill when I saw what I saw,' Bill's voice is soft, almost wistful, 'a lot of things went through my head…'

I grab other bits to wash up, keep my hands moving.

'That I might see May again for a bit, her spirit or something, I don't know. And I was that excited, like a nipper on Christmas Day, because I miss her so bloody much.'

I lift my hands from the soapy water and stare at the

picture of Bill and May, forever laughing, sadly parted. I think about Dad's picture at home, his smile stuck in time, and how much I miss him too.

The terrible pain of Dad not being here. Will it ever go? Do I want it to?

'But then, as I watched those girls disappear, I was suddenly afraid. Because even if I had seen her, May would go too, wouldn't she? Leave me again. And I was afraid of that feeling of loss, being greater than ever.'

I force back the tears before I turn.

'You understand, don't you, Sam?'

I can only nod, because I'm too sad to speak.

Oona draws closer.

'Sam, these things, these memories – they are as much your present and future as your past… they pass through the stone, like it's a projector on a screen.'

'Aye but you did something – how did you put it, "connecting the circle"?' says Bill.

Oona nods, strands of her dark hair falling.

'My mother taught me many things. How to channel, how to divine, how to see the magic in us all.'

I remember what Mrs Pratt said about her. *A devourer of divination.* Oona the white witch. The tarot reader. Priestess of the stone.

'Sam is seeing these things because they are raw in him, on the surface of his heart…'

'The stone once belonged to those witches – it still carries their essence – I believe they were the last to hold it, until Sam found it.' She smiles again. 'Or it found him.'

The clock ticks on, but time seems to have stopped and this kitchen is the centre of the universe.

'What about Odin, and my dad?'

'They are at the very centre of you, Sam. Your dearest memory, made real. Your father's favourite god, you said?' I nod, but I can't swallow anymore. 'Well then, the stone has carved you a door between myth and memory...'

'And Samhain is when it opens...'

Everything is suddenly connecting, the jigsaw pieces falling into place.

I look at Bill, and he looks at me.

'Not for me, lad. And that idiot in the car, he shouted something about the stone. What was that about?'

Dan snarls in my mind.

'He's just a lout. Doesn't mean anything.'

'It's all too rum for me, lad. Sorry.' He shakes his head.

And now with Bill apologising I can't help feeling angry. Why is he deserting me like this? I trusted him, telling him about the stone. And we're so close to something now.

'But I thought you'd want to help – you know, to make the circle...' I look at Oona, her black eyes shining. 'You'll be there, won't you, at the party?'

'Surely, Sam, but this is Bill's choice —'

I cut across her. 'What are you afraid of, Bill?'

'I said no, Sam. I'm sorry.'

'Oh stop apologising! Thanks for nothing, *mate*.' I'm

acting like a stupid spoiled kid, but that just makes me even angrier. 'Just sit here then and stew with your...' I move to the door quickly before the tears take me, and look back at his little kitchen, at his worried face.

'... your stupid old memories! And your stupid old dog...'

I slam the door behind me.

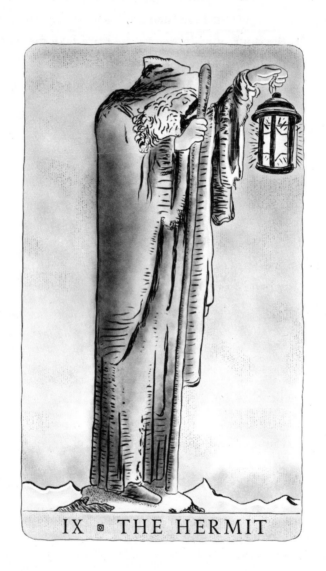

IX ◉ THE HERMIT

It's late afternoon when I get home.

I don't bother to turn on the lights. I just sit at the table. Alfie pads over, but I don't stroke him. I put my head in my hands, as the wind thumps the window.

Your stupid old memories!

Your stupid old dog!

That look on Bill's face. Why did I do that? Guilt grips me.

The lights click on, but I don't raise my head.

'Sam…'

I feel Mum's hands on my hair, on my hands, her warmth as she sits close.

'Has something happened, love?'

I start to laugh, but it comes out more like a gasp.

'Everything.'

Her hands gently pull mine away, and I let her, seeing her face. She looks better, rested. Like the further she gets from Dad's funeral, the more life finds her.

'And you're not going to tell me about it, are you?'

I shake my head. She strokes my cheek.

'You're so like your dad, you know.'

My father who wouldn't talk about the bad things, the fighting in the desert. Would always tell a joke, an old story, some piece of folklore he'd been reading. We all learned that this was the way that Dad would never bring darkness into our home. Perhaps that was right. Perhaps some things are best left good and buried.

'Okay, second question.' Mum's fingers link with mine. 'Did you talk to the doctor? About that call with your dad...'

'Mum, not again!'

I start to get up, but she presses me back. I'm too tired to fight.

'And like your dad to be *so* fuming with me? I mean, how awful is it? Such a strain! Ugh, Mum! Leave it, Mum!'

She rolls her eyes and gives big over-the-top sighs, playing grumpy me.

'Stop!' I can't help laughing at her teenager. 'I talked to her, all right. I did!'

She laughs too and it's good, suddenly, to be here with her, to laugh just because we can.

'I'm glad, Sam, I'm glad.' She takes my other hand. 'Because you know I've been feeling guilty too. And I've been thinking about the knots we get into...'

She smiles, but I can see the seam of sadness in it.

'I was cross with your dad too, you know… That he'd gone and left me… And I wouldn't be able to cope…'

'With me and Beth?'

She shakes her head.

'Sam, don't you see? It's because of you and Beth that I can. It's because of you, and everything your dad loved about you, that I see every day, that I think, don't wallow in this death thing, life's too short. It's over in a blink. All we have is this…' Her fingers stroke mine. 'The people we love, those we must keep close.'

My mother. My incredible, caring, one in a million mother. She's so wise, working her magic on me. My anger at Bill was selfish. I was scared. That things with the stone could be dangerous. Oona was right – it was Bill's choice. I was so wrapped up in my own feelings, I was blind to his.

I think about the time in the park, how he saw off Dan and his pack. I think about his denture-bright grin and wink, his 'daft apeth', his gruff kindness.

I draw away from Mum's hands.

'Hey, what did I say?' She looks crestfallen.

'All the right things.' I hug her and kiss her cheek.

'Well, isn't that the nicest thing to get from my son?' She beams at me. I will be hugging and kissing her as much as possible from now on. 'But where are you going, love?'

'There's something I need to do.'

'What?'

Mum and her barrage of questions. I'll never get sick of hearing them. They come from her fierceness, her protectiveness, from the deep earth of her love that built our family. I open the back door and smile at my miracle of a mum.

'To see someone I need to keep close.'

❋

Bill's street is quiet. I check my phone, where his icon pulses like a little heartbeat.

There are no lights on. But as I step to the front door the barking gets louder.

I knock gently. The dog barks faster, closer.

I knock again. Behind the glass, a shape moves and snorts.

'Badger?'

He whines and runs back into the darkness. I knock again. Nothing.

'Bill?'

I fumble for my phone, and quickly find his number.

It starts to ring. I edge to the window and try to peer past the net curtains.

'This is Bill Watson, I'm afraid I can't come to the phone right now, but...'

'Bill!' I tap on the window and Badger barks again. This doesn't feel right.

I head to the side of the house, through a wooden gate.

There's a door to the kitchen. I cup my face to the glass. There's the table where Bill sat. The photos on the wall. May smiling on the mountain.

'It's all too rum for me, lad. I'm sorry.'

I ring again, the cold of the window on my cheek. But no phone ringing, he must have it on silent.

And then I see something.

On the floor.

Bill's slippered foot.

'This is Bill Watson…'

'Bill!'

Badger barks.

I grab the door handle, surprised that the door swings open.

'BILL!'

I crash through the shadows, knocking a chair flat, nearly falling, throwing on all the lights.

Bill's motionless. Mouth open. A bottle of brandy, half drunk.

'Bill!'

I'm shaking him, Badger's pawing me, wagging his tail. Something falls to the floor. The picture of Bill and May laughing, full of love. No. No.

'No! Wake up!'

He groans. His hands are freezing.

'Bill, please wake up!'

'… Eh? Sam, whatsthis…?'

'I won't let you go! I won't!'

'Sam…?' He sits up with a cough.

His eyes are bright. He pulls me to sit, as my knees buckle.

'You all right, lad? You look shot.'

Badger's trying to climb onto my lap, but he's too old. He'll be dead soon, and Bill will have nothing, no one. And I can't help it, I start to cry, trying to speak through the pain. The terrible pain of nothing.

'Hey, lad… Hey now…' Bill's gnarled hands are on mine. Badger's watching.

'I thought…' I choke because tears are scalding my throat. 'I thought…' But I can't say the words.

Bill stares and a soft smile breaks across his face.

'You don't get rid of me that easy. Sam, I took a painkiller, is all. Just the one. And my old boiler's conked it, so I had a nip of brandy to stay warm. Right knocked me out. Next thing I know, you're here.'

I nod, trembling. The shock of him leaving me. He leans forward.

'You're here…' he says again, his smile growing. 'And it's good to see you.'

'It's good to be… to be…' It comes up through me, like a torrent, and I let it come because holding it back isn't possible. I can't do it anymore. I won't.

'Bill…'

I sob so much. For him stroking my hair.

'Hey now, Sam…'

'I'm sorry, Bill, I'm sorry, I'm sorry…'

I sob for everything that's gone wrong, that I can't change, that's just not fair.

'Promise me one thing...' he chuckles, whispering close, '*stop* apologising.'

For my friend who isn't dead, who didn't leave me. For a memory he's just soothed, without even knowing it.

'*It's all I have, son. I'm sorry.*'

'*I don't want your sorries either.*'

'Okay.'

For all the laughter and the sadness Bill draws from me.

'I promise. I promise...'

I get home, feeling shattered but happy. I can hear voices through our back door. I take a deep breath, ready for the Mum and Beth onslaught, and I open the door.

Chad and Beth are sitting at the kitchen table. He springs up.

'Sam! All right, buddy?! Blimey, you gave me a shock!'

A half-eaten sandwich lies on a plate. I grab it.

'Buddy?' I say through a mouthful of food. 'You all right?'

Chad laughs again, flicking his floppy hair. 'Yeah, yeah I'm good, all good...' he says glancing at Beth, who rolls her eyes. 'So... I popped round to see you, mate. What you been up to?'

What can I say to that? I've been watching spirits in the mist. I've been buzzed by lunatic Dan McGuire. I've lost and found a friend.

'Just out.' I shrug. 'So we meeting tomorrow night for the party?'

'Yeah!' says Chad, loudly, and looks again at Beth, who's lost in her phone, texting. 'We could meet up by the car park, about 9.30?'

'Sounds good.' I stifle a yawn, moving to the door. 'I'm beat...'

Chad's phone buzzes and he glances at it. He flushes.

'It's Darren... Just Darren. Er... says he'll meet us there too.'

His phone buzzes again, and he shoves it in his pocket with a laugh.

'Beth, you're coming, aren't you?'

She looks up from her phone, a big smile on her face. 'What? Oh... yeah, who isn't?' Then she jumps up and gives me a hug and I breathe in Beth. I've missed her.

'I've got a date,' she whispers, so only I can hear. A sister's secret.

'Can't wait to meet him,' I whisper back. 'He'd better be good enough for my Bethy.'

She laughs, her breath blowing my ear. 'He's better than good.'

'Get some rest, big night tomorrow.' She hugs me again, and Chad grins, watching us both. My best mate and my little sister, the people who know me through and through. I want to say more to them, but sleep is shutting me down.

Beth pushes me to the hallway.

'Up the wooden hill to Bedfordshire...'

'See you tomorrow, mate!' calls Chad as I make for the stairs. I wonder what it is that Beth says to make him laugh out loud. My sister, funnier than me.

But I'm too tired to think as, blissfully, I close my bedroom door and fall into bed.

XVIII ◉ THE MOON

'**S**am…' Oona's voice, low and lilting. 'Wake up, Sam.'

I do, and I see her, an eyebrow arching under her dark hair. We're sitting at a round table. I know where we are from the smell, that papery haven of the library.

Aisles of books stretch in every direction, like spokes of a wheel, we're the axle at its heart. The night is blue beyond the windows, where a tree waves black and willowy in the wind.

'Shuffle the cards, Sam.'

I look down at the deck in my hands, sifting the characters and symbols. I watch my hands move them, a kaleidoscope of colours.

Oona is spreading them around the table in a fan.

'Choose three…' she says. 'And give them to me.'

'This is a dream, isn't it, Oona?'

I make my choices, and I slide the cards towards her.

'Perhaps.' The queen of tarot places each card face down. 'Perhaps not...'

I look down the aisles. Nothing there. Yet I have a feeling that someone might be, someone watching, waiting in the shadows. Come out, come out wherever you are.

The sound of a card flicking over. 'The Moon'.

'This is your past, Sam...'

Two towers loom, and between them two dogs howl at the moon, that also seems to be the sun. There's a road, winding into the distance, and... is that a crayfish? It's scuttling from the water's edge, reaching up.

'It's a card of duality, of tension. One dog is like a pet, see.' She strokes its groomed back. 'The other, wild.' I meet its glaring gaze. 'Less a dog, more a wolf...'

The wolves that stalked my dreams. That ran howling through the mist.

'It's such a weird card...' I hear my voice. 'What does it mean, Oona?' I stare at that crayfish, clambering from the water.

'That we all struggle, Sam.' Her black eyes glimmer. 'That when there is little light to guide us...' she touches the sleeping moon, 'we must make hard choices...'

Footsteps sound along the aisle. Mrs Pratt come to turn us out.

'... to stay in safe water...'

But it's not Mrs Pratt. It's Mum and Beth, their arms around each other.

'... or face the difficult road.'

Oona's finger travels that trail into the darkness. She turns the next card.

'This is your present...'

A young man against mountain tops, a stick and bag slung over his shoulder, a little dog leaping at his side. The words beneath him make my belly twinge, because I know that's me.

'The Fool,' I say, my voice echoing, as more footsteps walk the aisles.

'Yes.' Oona studies his face, raised to the sky. 'The young adventurer with a head full of dreams...'

The footsteps stop, and I look up, perhaps knowing in my heart already who is there, as Rachel smiles beside Bill. He winks, of course, and turns to Chad, giving a thumbs-up.

'Fool he may be, teetering on the edge...'

Oona points to the cliff top at his feet. Does the young boy even know it's there?

'... but, unless he takes that step, leaps into the unknown, he will never make his way.'

I hold my breath as she moves to the last card.

More footsteps, the sound of something striking the floor. Closer and closer they come. And I know whose they are.

'This, Sam...'

Oona reaches for the card, as two girls, two true witches dance down an aisle. As Odin strides along another with his staff, his ravens, his wolves. As across the way, my dad saunters forward, looking up from his book to smile at me.

The last card is turning.

'… this is your future.'

She places it down, as the school bell rings and rings and rings.

I fumble for my ringing phone. Oona. Is she calling from the dream world?

'Sam, I've been ringing you for ages. It's the middle of the afternoon, you lazy lump.'

I feel groggy, as if I've slept a hundred years. It's dark outside.

'Are you okay?'

Seeing her in the library felt so real. I can feel the deck of cards in my hands.

'I… saw you in a dream. You were reading my cards. Three cards for my past, present…'

'And future,' she whispers, and I remember her turning that last card.

'Yes, but I didn't see it. I woke up.'

I can hear the smile in her breathing as she says,

'Shall I draw it for you now, Sam?'

'Yes… I want to know.'

I listen then to her breathing, her delicious breathing. I can hear the shuffle of cards.

'Tell me when to stop.'

I listen as they flick on, like the pages of a book where witches dance through time.

'Stop...'

She does and I bite my lip, I'm so tense.

'I'm going to send it to you.'

I switch to my phone's speaker, and hear Oona take a picture, the sound of the file sending. I imagine that card spinning across space, tumbling through the stars, fluttering down to my house, an owl on the wing, when my phone buzzes, and I open the message, the screen bright with the card, and I read that word, so small, so great.

DEATH

A knight with a skull for a face rides a white horse. Under a black flag, he strides over the body of a fallen king. There are people on their knees before him, a bishop, a maiden, a boy.

I think of Beth and me, of Dad carrying us on his shoulders, of us galloping to the White Horse.

'It's a card of change, Sam.' Oona's voice seems to make the picture glow and move. 'When the end is also the beginning. See on his flag, the ears of corn?'

I tear my eyes from Death's grin and look closer, the picture showing new things.

'It means the reaper brings the harvest. What we don't need is left behind, and what we do need, we keep to help us grow.'

As she talks, I see beyond that black standard, into the

distance where the sun peeps over the land, and it's as if Oona knows it too, can see into me.

'The sun is setting, Sam. But it's also rising. After death, there is life.'

I think of my dad waving from the hill, walking away into the light, following a figure with his birds and hounds.

'I went to see Bill…' My words are furry, clogged with sleep. 'We… we patched it up.'

'That's good. He was worried about you. We both were.'

I nod and look at the flyer that's been sitting on my bedside table this past month, reading the words I've read so many times:

HALLOWEEN @ THE WHITE HORSE

'Oona, will you meet me there tonight? At the party.'

There's a drawing of the horse jumping through a crowd of musical notes and lightning bolts. Beneath the spiders' webs and stars, something I hadn't noticed before, two smiling stick figures, hand in hand, dancing on the hill.

'Why, yes, Sam – remember, it's all us girls can think about.' Oona chuckles as I look at what's next to the flyer, waiting, watching, ready to fly.

The stone. The key to everything.

The stone has carved you a door between myth and memory…

And Samhain is when it opens…

'I have to do this, Oona, right? I have to try.'

'I know.'

'And you'll help me?'

'Both of you. You and your father.'

My phone buzzes. Chad.

PARTY TIME! WHOOP! WHOOP!

A series of emojis *ping, ping, ping.* A witch. An explosion. A running horse.

'Oona...'

'Time you got dressed.' Her voice swirls around me. 'I'll see you soon, Sam of Samhain.'

My phone goes dark.

From my bed I look to the door where my rented costume hangs, ready for action. The heavy jacket, the thick bottoms, the heavy boots.

Party time, Dad. It's party time.

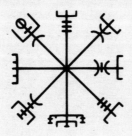

A month since we buried you.

You used to take me and Beth trick-or-treating when we were little.

Beth loved being a robot, all tin foil and cardboard, her huge grin peeping out.

Me as a little wolfman – you cried with laughter at my fierce frown. *Raar!*

The year we went as one big ghost – a bedsheet, six eyeholes, lots of giggles.

Now we're too old for that, of course.

Now we party with our mates.

But really, we'd prefer to put in the plastic fangs, drool fake blood.

Make a new monster

with you.

'Oh my word...'

Mum watches me, jaw dropping as the army's boots *clunk, clunk, clunk* on the stairs. 'Look at you, soldier boy...'

I turn to look in the hallway mirror, and she rests her hands on my camouflaged shoulders.

'Reminds me, you were always after putting your dad's uniform on when you were little, and now you're his size...'

I remember when he came home, that warm weight of his jacket, being folded into his smell. I remember slipping my toes into his giant's boots, as I searched his huge kit bag for treasures.

'Beth's gone on ahead.' Mum adjusts my beret. 'I think she's got a fella, you know.'

'What?'

'You'll catch flies in that!' she laughs, shutting my mouth. 'She's fifteen, Sam. Can't she have a bit of fun?'

'It's not that…' In the mirror I watch my cheeks burn. 'She just said she had a date. I didn't know she was seeing someone…' And why should I? This is the Beth who I normally told everything. The Beth who I didn't tell about the stone, or about seeing Dad. The Beth who had her things going on too, that she wasn't sharing with me. I watch the shame rise on my cheeks. I should be happy and excited for her, but I've really missed her, and now someone else is here for her.

Mum tugs my ear. 'And you can talk – what about this mystery girl? Oona, is it? When are you bringing her home to your mother, eh?'

The burning on my cheeks doesn't dim. I feel like a human lightbulb.

'I'm not sure, Mum. I'm not sure she likes me like that.'

I think back to the library, the picture of 'The Lovers' under our fingers.

How she shook mine, like she was shaking me awake.

'*Sam, we have things to do.*'

Looking at me, looking like Dad, I realise something. I've been wanting so badly for Oona to be mine, I want to show her off to Dad. I've been chasing the thought of her, as if she's some prize to be won, and she's so much more than that. I'm 'The Fool' indeed.

In the mirror, Mum watches the shame cross my face.

'You know, your dad was a pushy so-and-so, all flowers and chocolates and whatnot. And it was because I liked him so much and didn't want to lose him, that I kept things very slow. People need time and space, Sam. And as I told your dad, all good things come to those that wait.'

That makes me smile. Time and space, we're all travellers through it.

'You're so right, Mum.'

Something far off crackles, a PA system firing up. We hear the beat of music, drumming from the hill.

Mum opens the front door, letting in the cold.

'Sounds like things are kicking off up there...' She shivers. 'Brrr... you kids are nuts. In my day we'd be happy with a dance in the church hall.'

'Mum... I'll be late.'

I feel the weight of the stone in my jacket. If she knew, would she stop me?

I turn to go, when she pulls me back and hugs me tight.

'I'm so proud of you, Sam,' she whispers. 'You know that, don't you?'

I nod and the music from the hill calls through the night.

'And your dad would be too, you know that most of all, don't you?'

I nod again, and squeeze her hands.

'Go in, Mum. It's freezing.'

Finally, I ease from her grip and when I get to the gate, I turn to look at her, framed against the light. I think about how Dad must have felt, all those times he left on a tour. I think about the ache running through him, urging him to go back to her, to sweep her up and kiss her.

'Bye, my love. You have the best night, you hear?'

Her silhouette waves, and I leave at last, nerves kicking like crazy inside me, for what was coming, what waited up there on the hill.

'*Samhain,*' Oona whispers from a dream,

'*When all that's dead returns to the earth.*'

The crowd flows up the road, laughing and shouting. The lights from the hill seem to jump with the music. Everyone's hopping with energy and colour and life. Everywhere I look there's a sight. It's like a huge carnival. Our Halloween parade.

A gaggle of singing girls. They're dressed as pantomime witches. Green faces, black gowns and broomsticks. They pass, and I think about those true witches up on the plain, sisters in the mist. Would they come again tonight? Would Dad?

A gang of ghouls, arms around each other. Frankenstein's monster takes a selfie, a werewolf photobombs. Dracula hugs a bloody bride, his teeth on her neck.

My phone buzzes. It's Oona.

Sam, I'm up on the plain. Come find me ;-) X

'*Raaaa! Raaa! Raaa!*'

Skeletons hurtle by in black onesies, skull faces screaming,

'Let's hear it for Halloween, you horrible lot!'

The crowd hoots and cheers, and so do I, baying into the night. It feels so very, very good, urging us all to hurry. My phone buzzes. Chad, must be.

But it's not.

'Remember this?'

A picture of Bill's car skidded to a stop, our faces frozen.

Bodies bump, but I just stare, don't breathe.

'And this?'

Another picture. Our house, mud splatters on the window.

'Me want to party!'

A lad in a green buff suit barges me. More superheroes laugh as I twist around, the crowd tripping through the little carpark. So many people. My phone buzzes again. Chad.

Mate, we're waiting just past the car park entrance...

I try to type.

Then my phone rings. Enough of this.

'Dan, just leave it out, will you!'

There's a laugh, my heart jumps.

'Nice uniform. That your dead dad's?'

I look around. The crowd is pressing, everyone herding up the bank.

'Can't see me, Sammy boy? I can see you.'

'What do you want?'

Another call coming in. Oona trying to phone me.

'What do you think I want…?'

I stumble against the crowd, breathing fast, the music's louder and louder. And then I see the cowled figures under the trees. Grim Reapers waving their scythes at me. One holds a phone to his skull.

'See me now?'

I stop as the crowd streams past with shouts and laughter, whoops and cries. But I just watch Death's gang grinning.

'Going to be the party to end all parties, Sammy boy…'

I watch as Dan draws a bony finger under his skull throat.

'And you're on the guest list…'

I watch as they come for me.

XIII ◉ DEATH

I run through the darkness, up the hill.

My legs are on fire, my chest burns, but I run and run, because somewhere behind me there are Grim Reapers after my skin.

Shouts ring out, but I can't tell one from another, there are so many. In my clammy hand, my phone buzzes. It's Chad.

Where are you? Meet at the top. We're missing the dance!

Another shout behind me. Getting closer. No time to answer. I dare to look back.

Fluorescent figures dart in the dark.

They move faster than the roaming crowd. Because they're hunting. As I watch them weave nearer, the wind pushes across the hill, lifting the clouds, and a full moon shines down to find me. The crowd cheers.

'There he is!'

I duck into the wind, the grass drenching my legs as

I run. If I can circle around the high plain, perhaps I can lose them. There's something gleaming ahead. Where the White Horse lies hidden. I get closer, gulping for breath, and I see what it is.

All about the body of the horse, along each racing leg, down its arching back, a constellation of tiny lights, so the horse seems to leap across the stars. It's so beautiful that I want to stop and take it all in.

'Come on! He can't get far!'

But I can't stop. I have to run. My hand creeps to my pocket, for the only weapon I have. The stone curves under my fist. I'm not going down without a fight.

The ramparts loom ahead, lights sweep the sky. The PA squeals.

'Who's up for a dance tonight?'

Cheers upon cheers answer the DJ's call.

'Then let's get this Halloween started!'

The music swells, seems to shake loose from the earth itself. I risk a glance back. Skulls bob in the dark. I race forward, dropping between the banks, where I've been so many times, laughing with Beth, hiding from Dad.

I'm coming for you! Ready or not!

But now it's the reapers coming for me. I hear their breathing as I crouch, inching along the ditch. My heart pounds. They stop. And I see what they see through the banks, it's like a doorway to another world.

Light and smoke twist around dancing bodies. Hands fly in the air and mouths open, inhaling music.

Everywhere there's laughter and life.

'He must have gone in, come on!'

Cautiously, I creep forward, my fist tightening.

'Wait. Look that's his sister. In the wig.'

Bethy.

For a moment I can't see her in the crowd. All I glimpse is a young woman in flowing white, a gown that ripples around her as she spins like a dervish. Her dark hair flies, woven with tendrils of silver and gold. She's a witch goddess, summoning the crowd to bow before her. Bethy.

The reapers push into the noise, and I watch their black hoods disappear into the dancing. I've got to stay alert, anticipate Dan and his gang's next move. Got to wait for the right time. Got to find Oona. My eyes sweep the crowd.

Beth tugs someone towards her.

Hands circle her waist, as she turns and smiles.

As Chad pulls her into a kiss.

She breaks from him, fingers in his floppy hair, and over his shoulder our eyes meet. The music and the people have faded away. There's only me and Beth caught in this moment.

'*He better be good enough for my Bethy.*'

'*He's better than good.*'

Beth and Chad. My sister. My best friend. It was like the universe clicking into place. Suddenly everything made sense. She looks so happy, that I want to cry and laugh at the same time. My beautiful sister. If only Dad could see her now. If only.

Beth's eyes light as she smiles back at me through the crowd. She turns Chad around. He gives a sheepish wave. But their smiles freeze, as they shout.

'Sam!'

I'm flying forward, hitting the grass. Breath bursts from my lungs. The stone falls from my hand, into the dark.

'No!' I grab for it. 'No!'

'Yes! Found you!'

Four Grim Reapers look down at me. The largest steps forward, and in Dan's voice, Death yells.

'Time to dance, Sammy boy!'

'Sam!' Beth's there, pulling at me, but I'm stepping away.

The reapers stalk towards me, Dan's skull face leering.

'I said, dance, that's an order!'

They spring, shoving Beth to the ground.

'Beth!'

I grab for her, as agony shoots through my gut, and I'm on my knees, holding the spasm from Dan's punch. Shouts and screams.

'Leave him alone!'

'Stop fighting, you idiots!'

I can only see stars, trying to breath, trying to breath. Got to find the stone.

'Sam! Leave him alone, I said!'

And I look up, to see they've got hold of Chad.

'Look it's Pretty Boy.'

Two reapers laugh and throw him against Beth.

'Sam, I'm here!'

Oona's voice cuts through the blur of everything. She's dressed like Beth, two white witches against the night.

'I'll find the stone! Just run!'

But I can't run. I won't. So I picture the stone in my mind, reach for that surge of strength, as the music builds, as the crowd sways and bends.

'Get off him!'

They grab for me, I roll fast, and kick, my foot finding a soft landing.

One reaper crumples. Another takes his place, skull face glowing green, and I punch low, hearing its gasp as it plummets.

'Where are you, Dan?'

The crowd is a circle, a noise of faces and masks.

'Where are you?'

'Sam, watch out!'

I turn. Too late. Pain crashes into my head. Seering light.

Flash.

Flash.

Flash.

I stumble, want to vomit. Death raises his claw, curled about something hard. A stone of his own.

'I told you I'd give you a flamin' stone, Sammy boy!'

He swings and I duck, his fist flies close.

'Sam!'

Chad charges, but a reaper has him, and Death lets loose. Chad falls, red wringing from his nose. Fury makes me scream,

'YOU!'

I leap, like I did long ago, for the bully standing over my friend. But Death just laughs, and catches my throat.

'Hold him…'

Another blow to my belly. Sick in my mouth. I spit. They laugh.

Faces slide around me.

Death and white witches. A bearded giant.

Wolves, eyes glinting.

I saw them on the hill. I saw them with Dad.

'Dad…'

'He can't help you…'

A blow to my jaw, and blood fills my mouth. A dog howls.

'He's dead.'

Dad's turning to look at me. I can feel sunlight.

'Dan, what's that?'

I open my eyes to Death. There's such a light, such a bright light.

'One more for Sammy boy.' He looms, his fist draws.

'Dan, look!'

Witches, in a blaze of white. Their hands are joined. They lift the stone.

'They're coming, Sam! They're coming!'

I see Beth and Oona. I see two girls dancing through the mist.

I see something black, leaping, growling.

I see Dad, smiling at me.

'Run, Dan!'

'One more, I said!'

He strikes. A bomb in my head.

There's a door in front of me. Red sand on the window. An army truck.

'Sam... I told you I'd find a way.'

'Oona... I can see the door.'

Somewhere a siren sounds.

'The police! Run!'

I feel her hand on mine. I feel the stone between our fingers.

'Then open it, Sam,' she tells me from the shadows.

So I do.

'Hurry up, son...'

A big hand reaches and pulls me into the truck.

'Look sharp – you look like you've seen a ghost.'

Dad starts the engine. He swings the truck through the gates, past the sentries, out into the dusty road.

'Reckon he's just scared, sarge.' A soldier flicks my ear

so that I flinch round. Dan looks back at me with that leer, daring me.

'Let him be.' Another soldier shoves Dan back. 'Or you'll deal with me, understand?'

Dan drops his eyes, a scolded dog.

'Chad…' I say staring at my friend, sunlight on his narrow face.

'That's my name,' he smiles, 'don't wear it out.'

The truck rattles beneath me. I feel the warm metal of a rifle in my hand. There's sand on my lip. Through the open window I can smell the heat of the day where the bleached houses fly past, under a sky as blue as you like.

'Heads up.' Chad leans over. 'We're close.'

The soldiers are tense

'All right, lads. You know what's what,' Dad shouts over the engine. 'Market day is busy. The locals won't want us messing their sales. We make one circuit, and then we're through. What are we watching for, soldier?'

I blink at Dad. His eyes look into mine, waiting for an answer I don't have.

'Wake up, son.'

Dad swerves the truck. We're slowing, nearing a crowd. I can hear voices shouting their wares. 'People are here to buy and sell. I want eyes on anyone who isn't, okay?'

I nod. I reach for his shoulder.

'Da—'

Dad toots the horn.

'Move that animal, sir, would you kindly?'

A man peers through our window, dragging his mule along.

'Eyes and ears.' Chad taps my shoulder. 'We'll be home before you know it.'

The soldiers check guns, tighten straps, so I do the same, craning my neck to watch the looming houses, where a boy and a girl on a balcony look down as we rumble past.

'Here we go...' Dan grins, sweat trickling. 'Here we go.'

The truck turns a corner and people are milling everywhere, yelling and pointing. A woman holds a cage full of squawking chickens above her head. Boys cluster about a food stall, sweet smoke fills the truck. Piles of fruit and vegetables gleam in the sun.

The truck nudges along and heads turn to watch us.

Bare bulbs hang in dark shop doorways.

A gang of children, faces streaked with dirt, crowd about us, their begging hands reaching.

Chad throws a few coins, and we pick up speed.

The crowd is
thinning, the streets
seem quieter.

Ahead, a tall man steps from
the shadows. Birds flit above him, and thin
dogs slouch at his feet. He waves and waves. Dad slows,

'What's this now?'

Dan unclips his safety catch, his eye twitches.

It's a beggar, blind in one eye. He springs forward, his
hands groping for the door,

'You no be here!' he shouts, baring his broken teeth.
'Soldier go back! Soldier go back! Go back!'

'Thanks for nothing!' Dan shoves his hands away.
'Think we want to be here—?'

'McGuire, that's enough!' Dad silences him.

'Not here! Go back!'

'Clear out of it!' Dan snarls.

The beggar stumbles away. The dogs run beside the
truck, biting the wheels.

'Dad!'

But Dad doesn't hear as the truck roars away.
Something's not right. The dogs jump up.

'Get away, you mutts!'

'Danger! Go back!'

'Sarge!' Chad points at a tower of wooden crates in the
road. 'It's blocked, take a right!'

And I turn to glimpse the beggar, still waving, his dogs
howling like wolves.

'Dad, stop!'

'Hang on, it's blocked here too!'

He brakes hard, hauls the truck into reverse. But another car has closed in behind us. A man jumps out and runs, and we know, then, as we hear the sound of an engine roaring, as we hear wheels spinning in the dust. We know it's a trap, as we turn to see a van hurtle towards us.

Time slows.

Chad shouts, Dan goes for his gun.

We see the driver's face. He's young. Scared out of his wits.

I reach for my dad's hand and he looks at me.

Because I've got him, got him good.

When the van hits and the bomb explodes.

I feel grass under my fingers, beneath my head.

'Hey...'

Somebody's shaking me, gently.

'Rise and shine...'

I open my eyes.

'Found you, son...'

He pulls me to my feet.

I feel his hand on my chest. He's there. He's not a ghost. But still I shiver in the silvery light.

'Beautiful, isn't it?'

He turns to the dawn that prises the clouds from the earth. There's a smell of morning dew. It's as though the world has been washed clean, blown dry by the wind.

'Come on – the horse is waiting...'

We start to walk along the ridge, following a path between night and day. And above us, against the waking clouds, birds cry.

'Ravens, Sam. You don't see them about here much.'

I watch and the birds twist through a memory.

'Here she is…'

There's a line of white, chalk peeping from the earth. And that memory pulls me on, makes me laugh.

'But… I can't see it, Dad.'

He draws me close, remembering the same.

'Well now, there's the thing – the horse was made to be seen from far away, or from up high. I bet those birds have got a fine view.'

His hand is warm on my neck, and something makes me turn and look towards the old ramparts where an ancient fort once stood. Now there's only a tall figure against the sky. The wind lifts his long hair and two shapes crouch by their master's side. Odin, king of the gods, raises his staff and his wolves howl. I know we don't have long, I know my dad will have to go.

'Dad, I'm sorry—'

'*Shush*. I don't want your sorries, son.' And draws his arm across my shoulder and pulls me on, up those banks we've walked so many times.

He looks down into the plain, to the remnants of the party. The dancing has stopped, people are leaving in dribs and drabs, others linger watching the flashing blue lights.

'But that night, before… before the bomb.' I feel my throat close. 'I was so angry.'

'Sam…' He takes my face in his hands. The sky is in his eyes, where the ravens fly. 'Do you think that meant I

loved you any less?
Or that I thought you
didn't love me? In this great
and strange universe, do you really
think that mattered?'

He wipes the tear from my cheek and kisses the spot.
That feel of his stubble on my skin. It makes me cry
harder. He folds his arms around me.

'Forget guilt, Sam.' His laugh fills my body. 'All that
matters is taking care of yourself and those two...'

He points, and among a huddle I see Beth holding
Mum. They're kneeling next to me. There's a paramedic
and police.

'And watching out for your friends.'

There's Chad, and Oona. They're all there waiting for
me.

'That's all there is, son.'

I laugh out loud. 'Mum said the very same.'

The dawn lights his grin. 'Well now, we both know
not to argue with your mother.'

Beth shouts, the way she's always shouted, ever since
she could say the word,

'Sam! Sam!'

My heart pulls. I want to go to her, to all of them.

Dad points. 'You'll be in trouble, son, if you don't get
down there.'

But now I've got him, I don't want to leave him. There
are other figures, moving through the morning mist.

'Dad. Wait.'

He looks at me.

'I'm…' I force out the word, 'scared.'

'I know,' he says. 'Me too.'

I can see them dancing. Two girls, one small and dark, the other red-haired and fierce. Two true witches.

'But do you know how I know it's going to be okay, Sam?'

I shake my head.

'Because whatever happens, we're part of this place for ever.' Dad holds my shoulder. 'Us and the horse, the land and the sky.'

The wind lifts and blows those witches back through time.

'Sam!' Beth's voice echoes across the plain.

For a moment I want to join Dad, run along the ramparts, where the tall figure waits.

'Sam!'

My heart soars as my dad turns to me.

'I love you, Sam. More than salt.'

He's following Odin now beyond the rise, as a raven flies up up up, and I think of that day we buried him and all seemed lost.

But nothing really was. Everything was here all along. This day is that day.

Give him a wave, then, Sam – perhaps he'll bring us luck.

That day I couldn't, wouldn't. This day I can. I do. I

say my goodbye to you.

I feel like that bird rising on the wind, feel its shout, seeing the land all around.

'Sam! Come back to me!'

My sister, my mum, my friends.

Seeing something I've always wanted to see. It makes me laugh,

'I see it, Dad! I see the horse!'

And we watch as the raven flies over that great white horse ever galloping across the hill.

Then with a cry of joy it dives.

Down.

Down.

Down.

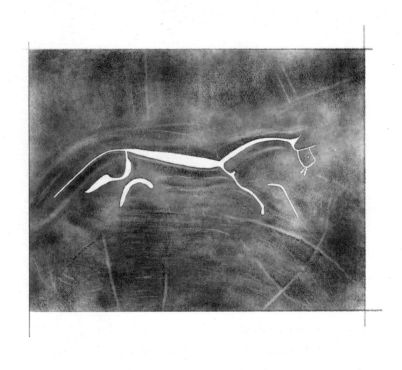

'**S**am?'

I open my eyes to a huddle of faces. Beth. Mum. Oona.

'Hey…' Mum's hand is soft on my cheek. 'Who's been in the wars, eh?'

The blue light of a police van flicks across the plain. I can see a policewoman writing as Chad talks and gestures. He catches my eye and smiles.

'Come on, lad…'

There's a paramedic in green high vis. He starts to put his arms under mine.

'Wait, I'm okay.' I sit up and they all watch me, as if I'm about to break. 'I'm fine.'

'Love,' Mum squeezes my arm, 'they need to check you over.' Another paramedic is by my side. She nods and waits.

'He'll go with us, won't you, Sam?'

Beth puts her arm around me, her laser-green eyes full of dawn light.

'He will, if he knows what's good for him.'

Oona takes my hand and they lead me, those white witches, step by step to the back of the ambulance as the sun starts to peep above the ridge. It feels like a hundred years have passed.

'Follow the light, son.'

'What's that?'

The paramedic holds a little torch.

'With your eye – follow the light.'

'Look up,' says the paramedic, and I laugh again, touching Beth's head with mine.

'So, Chad, then?'

She looks over at him talking with Mum and the policewoman. Beth waves and he waves back. Something in me shifts. Things have changed. She's still my little sister, he's still my best friend. But they're their own people with their own dreams, finding each other, liking each other. Beth and Chad together.

'Yeah. Told you he was the best.' She shoulders me, as I knew she would. 'So, you guys, then?'

I feel Oona's closeness, the warmth of her hand on mine, and Mum's words echo. *All good things come to those that wait.*

'Perhaps...' I smile, remembering 'The Lovers' in the library.

'You're okay, son.' The paramedic says. 'Just take it easy, all right?'

'Thank you. We'll make sure he does.' Beth and Oona

walk me gently away. I feel the dull ache of a punch in the ribs. Death had a mean jab. 'Surrounded by females is the best, eh, Sam?'

I nod. 'The best.'

Somewhere up the hill, a dog barks. I shield my eyes to peer up.

'Someone's up there, Sam. Can you see?'

I follow Beth's finger and there, standing against the dawn, is a figure.

'Give him a wave, then.' Beth laughs and shouts out, 'Hello, hello!' She raises her arm to wave, and the man on the hill waves back. It's like a waking dream.

The dog barks louder and closer. I know that bark.

'Here, boy! Here!'

Then Badger comes tumbling into our legs, whining and licking, and I look again at the figure waiting on the hill.

'Go on, then.' Beth gives me a shove. 'I'll catch you up. Now, Mr Badger, how are you?' She kneels to pet the old dog that snorts and wags his tail madly for her.

'Here, Sam...' Oona moves something to my hand.

The stone. I had forgotten all about it.

'You found it on the hill after all,' she says, her voice lifting and lilting as I touch that familiar notch, the weathered grain, the centuries of stories. 'Who will find it next, I wonder?'

She smiles her witchy smile, and I grin back at her.

'Will you wait for me?'

'Why surely, Sam.'

She curtsies and laughs and I hug her quickly, warmly. Then I turn and walk across the plain, letting the wind take me. As I grip the stone, that figure seems to change, turning in the light, becomes one and many things.

A god called Odin.

A little girl called Dill, dancing in the day.

A soldier called Alan Mitchell, sergeant in the 2nd Battalion The Rifles. My dad.

An old man, leaning on a stick.

For a moment we stare at each other under the clear blue sky.

'It's good to see you, Bill.'

'Isn't it just?' He winks then looks me over. 'Looked like a cracking party.'

I feel the bumps and bruises. 'I think I'm done with parties for a bit.'

He laughs and loops his arm through mine as we walk along the ridge.

'You know, you've gone and done it now, don't you?'

'Done what?'

'Got me hooked on this place, and on—' He stops, his breath clouding as he squints through the sunlight. 'And on you lot. You won't shake me off now, you know.'

I match his grin. 'Oh dear.'

Below us, Beth throws a stick for Badger who just sits and looks at it.

'So I shall come here to walk. It's high time I got off

that bench and got some air into me lungs.'

'Can I come too?'

'Of course, you're to blame for all this exercise!' Bill smiles. 'And besides, you've got all the stories. All those myths and legends, eh, lad?'

Above us a bird turns, banking above the hill where the White Horse leaps. I can see its huge eyes, those speckled wings.

'So what now, what about that stone of yours, Sam?'

I open my hand and we look down at it, as I turn it, watching those tiny silver grains like stars, a galaxy in my palm.

I raise my arm and the owl plunges.

'It's not mine anymore.'

I hurl the stone, send it flying, up, where the owl seems to curl about it.

Bill gasps, as the bird banks into the blue, and I know, whatever it was, the stone is done with me, and I with it.

I look down to where my sister waves at me, and shows Badger to Chad and Mum. I look to where Oona is waiting.

'Sam, lad, you know what you are, don't you?' says Bill. 'You, young man, are one daft apeth.'

And we walk together, across the hillside to the White Horse.

The raven lands heavily. There's a worm in its beak. The last of the leaves are falling from the horse chestnut tree. The bare branches move in the wind, pushing and pulling, until the raven takes wing, blinking black, white, black, white, and it's gone, and there's only Rachel saying,

'And after that, Sam, what happened?'

I think back over the past few days. Waking to see Beth, Oona and Mum, the crowd of strange faces and masks, like characters from a deck of cards. I remember the throb of my head, the ache in my jaw.

'Mum was there – Beth phoned her. And the police, paramedics…' My voice trails into a blur of flashing lights, shouts, strong hands lifting me.

'It must be good to have a little sister always looking out for you.'

I remember Beth and Oona, their hands linked, white witches against the night.

'Yeah. She's a right pain.'

I try to smile but my jaw just makes me wince. Rachel watches me, and I realise I've missed her steady gaze, being in her still room with the great tree at the window.

'I hear the police know those boys, from the fight.'

I remember Death grimacing, rising to strike. But something came running, black and quick.

'Thank goodness for their dogs scaring them off.'

'Yeah.' I nod, as Odin's wolves pad away into gloom. 'Alsatians are scary things.'

I look up at Rachel, waiting, as if she's offered me her hand, to climb the great hill together.

'Sam, the last time you were here, you said you were going to find your father, to bring him back?'

'Yes.' My voice becomes a whisper. 'I found him…' as soft as Oona's breath on my cheek. 'And let him go.'

Rachel leans closer. 'You sound reconciled, Sam. At peace.'

I look up at her, with her gentle way, that grey gaze that waits to draw the ache from me. But there's none to give.

'I am, Rachel. I am.'

I laugh as my tears run. I keep laughing as I reach for that box of tissues, waiting so patiently all this time.

'They got me in the end, eh?'

Rachel nods, as I pick at them. Now I've started, I can't stop.

'You've come a long way.'

I wipe my eyes. 'Doesn't mean I want to stop coming here, though.'

She smiles, surprised.

But I mean it. It's not something I think she wants to hear. I want to come and sit with this wise, funny person. I want to drink her tea and talk about anything. To see the tree turn through the seasons, that little circus dog forever running on his ball.

'I'm glad, Sam. Who else would I chat to about myths and fairy tales and—'

'... death?'

'Yes.' Rachel smiles. 'And life, Sam. Death and life.'

My tears have stopped. For the first time in a long time I don't feel scared, or angry, or down. I feel free as a bird in a winter sky.

Beep, beep

Rachel taps her watch.

Right on cue. I rise from the armchair. There's a buzz in my belly. I'm excited, about what's out there, waiting for me in Dad's great and strange universe.

'Until next time, then, Sam.'

'Yeah. Until next time.'

And I open the door.

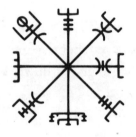

AUTHOR'S NOTE

I was in my early twenties, a few years older than Sam, but I think still teenage in spirit, when I was confronted by death. A friend and mentor lost their life, suddenly, tragically. And however hard I ran through that long dark night, I couldn't bring him back. Afterwards the days and weeks passed in a haze of shock, confusion and anger. I was in a different place, and the world would never be the same again.

I began having panic attacks. I couldn't cope. Bleak thoughts scared me. I needed to get help. I started to see a psychotherapist who specialised in bereavement counselling. For a while, things got worse before they got better. Death was just so unfair, I couldn't accept it, and it seemed to taint everything. But over time, through these sessions, I started to see that death wasn't something I could control. The pain of that loss was part of me now, and life had to go on. Psychotherapy is an incredible thing. If you are suffering, for whatever reason, protect your mental health and find someone who can help you.

Sam's interest in the 'deities of the dark' is one much of humanity shares. For some, the end is nothingness, for others it is the next stage of a journey. Do we have souls? Is there a spirit world? We'll find out one day. In the meantime, like Sam, we need to make the most of what we have, love and look after each other.

And laugh as much as possible.

ACKNOWLEDGEMENTS

There are always many people who help bring a book into being. I could not have written *Stone* without their inspiration, support and creativity. First, thank you to my sister, Sally, who bought me a week at the Arvon Foundation's wonderful Lumb Bank centre.

Thank you to Lucy Christopher - this story started in her writing workshop and I still have all my notes. Thank you to the writer friends I made there, in particular Kirsty Applebaum, Maddy Woosnam, Helen Lipscombe and Sally Purdie. Thank you to my other Arvon tutor, Melvin Burgess, for all his enthusiasm, regardless of my broken-down car. Thank you to Meg Rosoff for her inspiring talk about the writer's imagination - a version of her story has found its way into these pages.

Thank you to Chris Vick, who encouraged me on my return from Hebden Bridge, and has helped this book grow over the years.

Thank you to Emma Feasby for her psychotherapy advice and loan of the books on Carl Jung.

Thank you to my agent, Catherine Pellegrino, for her tireless support and good humour.

Thank you to my publisher, Fiona Kennedy, for her editorial brilliance, wisdom and cups of tea in her kitchen. Thank you to Meg Pickford and Jon Appleton and all the awesome team at Zephyr who have made Stone such a beauty, particularly Jessie Price and Clémence Jacquinet in Art and Production. Thank you to Edward Bettison for his corking cover design. Thank you to Laura Smythe for her publicity prowess.

Thank you to my parents, Colin and Jacqui, for always cheering me on. Thank you to my patient, loving family, Abby, Molly, Sam and my furry muse, Coco. Thank you to my grandparents, dearly departed, the spirits of them all are woven into this book.

And thank you to Michael, wherever you are, for all the teasing and laughter.

Finbar Hawkins
Bath
June 2022

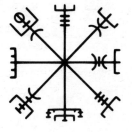

WITCH

FINBAR HAWKINS

OUT NOW

I never did no magick.

Not at the time they said, anyways.

It was Mother who heard them. Mother could hear a frog hiccup from a mile yonder. She could whisper out a blackcap nesting in the trees. Mother had old ways, from far across the sea. And that's what she looked to teach us. Perhaps that's what led to it all. All the blood. And the death.

When Mother hollered us, I didn't see them. Dill pointed down.

'There, Eveline, there low!'

I saw them. The skulkers. Men. Horses. They were coming. They knew us.

No matter that Mother healed them. Cured their stock. Smacked their children into the world. Here they came, like whelps. Boys to fetch us in. Scared. Angry. Men.

'Dill, get!'

We ran fleet foot, wind after catching us, and we found Mother, leaning on her staff. She pressed a bag to me. She was pale as birch bark. She could not run. Her leg was twisted and scarred like a root grown wrong.

'They're coming!' Dill pulled at Mother, who only bent to stroke dirt from her cheek.

'Here, my Dilly Dee...'

She opened Dill's hand to place something. It sat round and black and heavy on Dill's thin fingers. The Wolf Tree Stone. Mother's scrying stone. Then she looked me sharp.

'Get to the coven. Find my sister. Look to Dill. Go now!'

I remember that. Her face like wax settled on wood. Her lips split. Her eyes all fire.

'Evey, swear you will ever look to Dill.'

Her face so fierce with love. I heard shouts. They were close.

'For my blood, your blood, your sister's blood...' She pushed against me. 'Swear it and go, Evey!'

And this I have of her always. Her mouth, shouting, furious at me.

'I do swear it, Mother...' Then I took Dill's hand and we ran.

We ran to the near wood. Like rabbits before the dogs. That's what they were, see. Not men, but dogs that stank and slavered. We made the trees when I heard a shriek that shanked deep as a knife.

Dill wanted back, but that wouldn't be. She pulled at me, kicked and scratched. Mother let shriek again. I remember her cry, like a fox snared.

'Evey, they're hurting her... EVEY!'

But I held Dill fast. She gripped Mother's stone, her fingers tight white.

'Hush it, Dill – we'll be caught.'

There were four of them. They had broken her staff. They had ripped her dress. Mother brought her arm to her breasts, as she swayed upon her good leg, her dark hair flying, her eyes coals in the fire.

I knew then. She saw her end.

And in that moment, she saw theirs.

'Touch not my children!' Her voice echoed to the watching sky. 'Or I swear it, you all...' She pointed at the four who watched her. 'You all will die!'

She was so strong, so beautiful, so alone.

Then one came close and struck her face.

I felt it like he struck my own. I stopped my mouth from crying out.

Mother fell.

How I wanted to run to her. Swing high to skewer those dogs. But I had no blade. They were too many. And I would break Mother's bond.

Go, Evey. For me. For Dill.

My sister twisted like a wild cat. But I held her good, as a tall one turned about, as if he caught our scent. Quick I pulled Dill lower as she moaned over.

'Mother, Mother, Mother...' Her fingers pulling at mine.

And my guts churned with shame for our hiding, as I marked him, this Tall One with his long black hat. He raised his arm high, like as to hail me. Then let it fall, and his men sprang to. Laughing, shouting, they lifted Mother, as she struggled in their grip.

I couldn't go. They were too many.

Evey.

They brought Mother to the ground and laid her arm. And the largest, he ran and he jumped, like a boy at play. He jumped and snapped her arm. That sound, breaking like an old branch in the wood where we hid. He snapped her arm. And Mother shrieked and rolled as they laughed like dogs. Like men.

They closed around her. I could not see.

Please.

Four men.

For me.

They beat her.

For Dill.

Over and again.

Go. Now.

Then I felt it.

I could not run to her, but I could curse them.

So I did. I cursed them with all my fury.

'Know this, I will not rest till balance got.
Till time turned back. Till light be sought.
Till dogs be dirt and death be done.
Till then. Only then, know this.'

I held Dill's face to my chest, away from their blows.

They shouted with glee. They pushed her down. Still she raised to her knees, her arm hanging as a spider's thread broken in the breeze.

'My children!'

Her voice echoed, so that I will ever hear it. There was stillness and there was Mother and the men and us watching and our hearts beating.

Then another stepped forward. He was young, not yet a man. He raised his musket high.

Mother looked up to this brave boy. She spat.

He swore and swung that musket so swift and smote her skull. She rolled, then did not move, in the mud.

And we knew Mother was dead.

'No. NO!'

Dill pushed at me, crying, but I grabbed her mouth. She was little then. She wasn't strong much. Fast like a cat, but light as a bird was Dill.

'Shush, or we'll be got!' Pain tore my voice. 'Shush, now, Dill, you... you hear!'

Dill's tears ran over my hand, her eyes screaming. Yet she nodded, as she shook.

They were standing about Mother. Voices low, butchers weighing a pig. Some pissed. Like dogs. Like dogs. Then Tall One pushed and shouted at that brave boy who killed our mother.

'The witch was for trial, boy! We still have not the children!'

I felt cold creep across my body, my hairs standing. They knew us, sought us. The brave lad shouted back, for he was not afeared.

'You saw – she cursed me! You have to kill 'em quick so it will not take!'

He spat upon Mother and kicked her withered leg. I fought to snatch Mother's stone from Dill and run to him and smash his face. But I could not, I could not.

'Find them!' Tall One turned to that thin man, that heavy brute, that brave lad, all those dogs who I marked true. 'Find them now!'

We had to fly, Mother.

I cursed them and cursed them good. Everything you gave me, I gave to them.

Tall One roused his pack towards the woods.

We flew for our hearts.

We flew for you.

We were running in the dark wood, Dill close to.

Little she was, but she could fly all the same. Time past I chased her tawny legs through summer's dusk. When we ran as sisters not as rabbits, feared for our skins.

We fell to a stream, cupped our faces, drinking deep. Then we stood in the running water. Far-off shouts now, not near. Those dogs were slow.

A sparrow flitted to a branch above, and cried, *This way, this way, this way.* Dill breathed hard as she listened. The stream pressed cold about our feet. We saw ourselves in the water. Dill, skin and bone, pale as morning milk, her hair black and thick as a rook's nest. And me taller, my cheeks, my arms all mottled over, like drops of brown rain, my hair long and red. The colour of anger, Mother used to say. And the song she sang for me, came babbling through that green water.

'Evey Red Braid,
watch thy mist.
Evey Red Locks,
drop thy fist.'

Dill smiled to the girls in the water. The younger waved to see her. But her sister frowned and said, 'Silly mite. This is not the time for playing. Come now.'

We brooked the stream, smooth stones under foot and held at roots to make the bank. I listened true. No dog came barking. Dill's hand was soft and small as a mouse in mine. We passed through the wood, and after a time, we saw it, sitting far away, smoke lifting, like hair in the wind.

'Why there, Evey?' She pointed to town with her fist curled about the black stone.

'Because that's where dogs will home to sleep.'

And I swear, Mother. I never will let them lie. Only in death.

Only then.

EmpathyLab

ZEPHYR

We are an Empathy Builder Publisher

- Empathy is our ability to understand and share someone else's feelings
- It builds stronger, kinder communities
- It's a crucial life skill that can be learned

We are supporting **EmpathyLab** in their work to develop a book-based empathy movement in a drive to reach one million children a year and more.

Find out more at www.empathylab.uk
www.empathylab.uk/what-is-empathy-day

Zephyr is an imprint of Head of Zeus.
At Zephyr we are proud to publish books
you can read and re-read time and time
again because they tell a brilliant story
and because they entertain you.

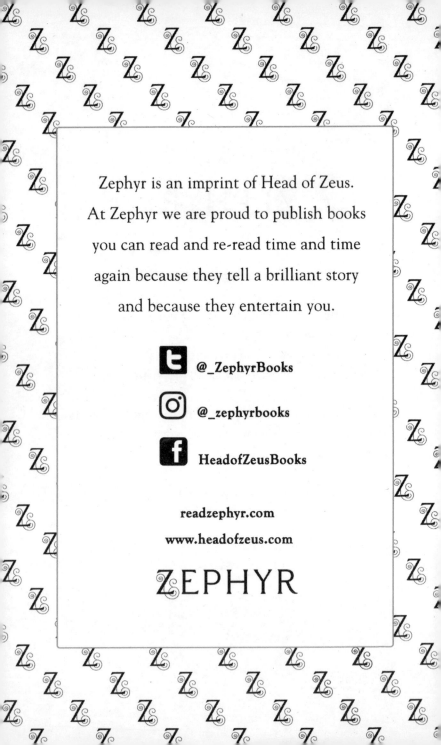 @_ZephyrBooks

@_zephyrbooks

HeadofZeusBooks

readzephyr.com

www.headofzeus.com

ZEPHYR